RETURN
TO
THE
DIRT

Geoff Sturtevant

Disclaimer:

This is a work of fiction. Names, characters, businesses, places, events and incidents are either the products of the author's imagination or used in a fictitious manner. Any resemblance to actual persons, living or dead, or actual events is purely coincidental.

THE
TECHNICIANS

1

Technician one: "How's it going?"

Technician two: "Eh, can't complain."

Technician one: "Another day in paradise, eh?"

Technician two: "Another day, another dollar."

Technician one: "Eh, waddya gonna do, right?"

And so on. It's enough to make you vomit. And coming from a guy with a job as utterly disgusting as mine, those are strong words.

For all the useless things I learned in school;

Geometry, Chemistry, Trig, Trig 2, Chemistry 2, etcetera, they never taught me what I really needed to know. Why? Because the world was our oyster. Truth is, there are two ways an average guy can make a living wage these days; to do a job other people *can't do,* because their papers don't say they're qualified to do it, or a job other people don't *want* to do. The can't-dos are for the college grads with the insight to enter the fields that fit the jobs of the age. The don't-wanna-do's are for guys like me; guys who thought their studies would give worth to their futures, rather than their futures giving worth to their studies. Guys who expected great, big pearls to fall out of that proverbial oyster and land in their laps. So here I am, a college graduate, listening to this prattle, the dullard's morning mantra. Waddya gonna do *indeed.*

Me, I'm 35 years old, a veteran of decent-paying, don't-wanna-do jobs. At some point, I found myself providing for a wife and four-year-old twin girls. It all snuck up on me like a terminal illness. The wife lost all respect for me long ago. The girls are too young to lose respect for me yet, but they'll learn to

3

in time. Your efforts to be a provider may initially entitle you to some appreciation, but this rule is written in water. Observe, youngsters; there are no oysters. There are no pearls. Or as Oscar Wilde might have told you, the world *was* your oyster, young millennials, but you used the wrong fork.

My partner Fernando is another one of us don't-wanna-dos, but he happens to be an exceptional one. I spend a great deal of my day with the guy. He's a character, always smiling and shaking his head the way he does, as though the more absurd it all gets, the more amused he is. The accent is good too; that kind of unabashed Spanish accent where r's are rolling all over the place. Really, you gotta like the guy. 44 years in the books, still fighting to be good-natured. He still cares about stuff; the quality of his work, his family life, getting home for what he calls "love night" on Wednesdays. Love night is sacred to Fernando. I respect it. But I can't relate to it.

For a lowly tech like myself, Fernando does some inspired work. "If a man is called to be a street sweeper, he should sweep streets even as a Michelangelo painted, or Beethoven composed

4

music or Shakespeare wrote poetry, etcetera"—that was Martin Luther King Jr, talking about my partner Fernando. Yes, I know, Fernando, "me and my quotes." Now that I'm a street sweeper myself, I like that one a whole lot less than I used to. Still, I'm lucky to work under the tutelage of the Great Fernando. Stand on the shoulders of giants, isn't that what they say?

Once we get out of the building and onto the road, we have an alright time together. That's really all you can hope for; to have an *alright* time. "Waddya gonna do," you ask? Here's the answer: follow the 43 methods, have an alright time, and go fart in your lunchpail.

It's the middle of May. There's a haze of pollen on the windshield where the wipers can't reach. That constant itch in the crooks of your eyes; right in the armpits of your eyes. And that faint feeling in the back of your throat like you're getting sick all the time. Springtime in New Jersey is the drizzling shits. Fernando, chipper as always, seems to be immune to the pollen. Maybe it's that little mustache of his that filters it out. So, we're on the turnpike, 9:20 in the morning, me and my partner in crime.

"So your mom is Jewish, or your dad is Jewish?" asks Fernando. His little mustache is crooked again this morning. He always manages to shave one side a little shorter than the other, just enough so I end up staring at it with mild irritation over lunch. For a guy so detail-oriented, his mustache-maintenance is haphazard.

"My mom is Jewish," I say. "Was Jewish."

"You *mom* was Jewish. So that means you're Jewish."

"That's what they say."

"You don't look Jewish, meh." He glanced over to confirm his suspicion.

"Eyes on the road, Fern. And you're right, I don't look Jewish. I've got that going for me."

"Why's that, what do Jews look like, meh?"

"You just said I don't look like a Jew, so you must have some frame of reference."

"Eh, big nose, afro hair, stuff like that, right? Hairy?"

"Sounds like you, Fern."

Fernando looks down at his hairy arms. "My Gah.

I'm the Costa Rican Jew..."

The GPS says to take Pembroke Avenue. Fernando taps at the screen. It's been awhile since we were down this way.

"So what are we doing in this shitty truck?" I ask.

"Going to work, meh."

"Very funny. I mean what are a couple of Jewish boys doing driving around in a shitty truck without air conditioning? We're supposed to have those suit-and-tie jobs, aren't we?"

"Someone's gotta do the real work, bro." He billows the heat from his shirt.

The only thing separating you from the heat of the engine in these trucks is a plate of aluminum, which gets to approximately the temperature of the sun. The heat from the diamond plate flooring goes right through your boots. Some mystery-bolt tinks from the undercarriage and spins in the wheelwell and rolls down Pembroke Avenue. I hear it all the time. One day some important bolt will fall off and we'll go rolling down the road ourselves.

"So how's the family?" asks Fernando.

"The family. Fine, I guess. Kids are fine."

"That's good, meh."

"Yeah. Kids are fine."

"How old are they again? Four?"

"Just turned four."

"Man. Time flies, bro."

"No kidding."

"How about you and the Mrs?" asks Fernando.

"Who knows."

"You gotta stay good with her, bro. Gotta work at it, know what I mean?"

"Yeah, yeah. I know what you mean, but come on already...I give her all my money, isn't that enough?"

"Nah, bro. You gotta give it to her. Gotta give *it* to her, meh." He does his best humping gesture from a driving position.

"Give *it* to her? she doesn't want *it,* trust me."

"Man..." He shakes his head. We've been through this a million times—at least every Wednesday. The guy just isn't ready to give up on me.

The engine backfires and another mystery-screw tinks in the undercarriage. A hispanic guy watches from the curb. I meet eyes with him in the mirror, then he's gone.

Fernando mercifully changes the subject: "Hey, you know they're bothering me to get new uniforms again?"

The pleats in my polyester work pants are still crisp. Fern's are worn paper-thin, several shades lighter red than mine, save for the faint stains the original color was intended to hide. It takes a lot of washes to get these heavy-duty work clothes worn comfortably thin, and he'd turned away every uniform requisition form for nearly a decade.

"Haven't they for years?"

"Yeah, they never learn, bro. Look at this meh, look how thin it is." He pinches his sleeve between thumb and forefinger. You can see the light through it.

"Yeah, I know, you've showed me."

"Gotta stay comfortable, meh. I dry clean these. If I put them in the washer, I'm afraid they'll fall apart."

"You dry clean them?"

"Yeah, meh. Isabella thinks I'm crazy."

"I think she's got a point."

Fernando chuckles. "That's messed up, meh, you're supposed to be on my side here." He slaps my thigh.

"Didn't feel it," I say, "my pants are too thick."

"See that, meh? I told you. Your balls are gonna be sweatin!"

Observe, youngsters, that's what I took away from my college education. Sweaty balls.

The GPS says to stay right at the fork. In another mile, we'll make a left on 13th Street. In another five miles is North Ave, then Maple Street. That's where the job is.

Fernando glances over. "So you gonna lead this one meh?"

I look at him, mid-yawn. Suddenly, I'm not so tired. "The lead? You mean...I wasn't planning to."

"Gotta do it sometime, you know?"

I consider it a moment. A million scenarios run through my mind, all bad ones. "Why don't we have a look first? We don't need to decide now."

"Man, what a rookie. Big, small, same thing, you know that."

"Yeah, so they say."

But this is veteran thinking, that size isn't a factor. I tend to think if you haven't quite mastered the finesse that only comes with years of experience, you're probably better off learning in more forgiving conditions. This is greenie stuff, admittedly, but after eight months, I'm still pretty green. And come on, I'm not supposed to be a technician. I'm supposed to be a novelist. Or a professor. Something like that.

"You know how it is," I say. "Let's not play make-pretend idealism."

"Yeah, yeah, I know. Alright, we'll check it out first."

I'm yet to lead a job. The first guy I'd partnered up with was a seventeen-year vet who'd since retired. That was an easy one though; an old lady whose alarm didn't work. All we needed was a wire. The next was with Fernando, also a disabled alarm, and all we needed was a screwdriver. Still, I'd been nervous. It takes time to make all the methods second-nature, and this is critical for the split-second decisions needed to improvise on the go. It's a principle of the job.

Methodology, principle #3:
Improvisation in unexpected conditions.

Making quick decisions and executing them correctly depends a lot on these details. Same as a painter would tape carefully over woodwork, or a carpenter would measure twice before cutting a board, Fernando's experience is most obvious in the job's subtleties, including his own finicky, little preferences. His insistence on a soft, worn-out uniform shirt, and thin-soled sneakers. Steel-toed boots were the industry standard, but "you can't feel your feet on the ground," he'd explained to me, "important for leverage and control." He even takes the insoles out of his shoes. Fernando isn't exactly a physical specimen; he relies heavily on technique— also a principle of the job. The first, in fact.

Methodology, principle #1:
Technique first. (also commonly described:
technique, technique, technique.)

We pull up to 5664 Maple Street at 10:05 a.m.

"Alright, so what do we have here?" asks Fernando.

He hadn't even glanced at the work order. With experience, the techs become comfortable enough to walk into a job cold, confident they can handle whatever it is. They constantly drill it into our brains to always be prepared, but veteran guys like Fern seem to rely more on their instincts. I typically won't give him any info besides the address until we get there, and he decides our approach on the spot.

Flustered as always, I fumble through the itinerary to find some specifics.

"Alright, here it is: Harold Chapman, 5664 Maple Street...says he's expecting the carpet cleaners. Big wine stain in the living room. Shit, we got the carpet cleaner, right?"

"Yeah meh, we're all good."

"Alright. So that's all I got."

"Remind me to thank dispatch for the generous details." He releases his seatbelt. "So what do you think? You wanna try it or what?"

My heart starts going. It always did to some degree, but now it was *really* going.

"I dunno man, maybe not. I'll backup."

"Man, you gotta try soon, you know?"

"Yeah, I know," I say. "Now isn't the time, there's no description or anything. I know what you're

gonna say—size doesn't matter—but I'd rather
know."

"Okay, just really pay attention, alright? Gotta
learn something new every time."

"You got it, Fern."

"Alright, meh."

He checks the mirrors, then opens the door and
rolls out. Fern isn't exactly a fat guy, just strangely-
proportioned, like a big bowling pin. He walks like
one too; a goofy, waddling way about him that might
lead you to believe he can't move the way he does.
But when he needs to, he can really move.

I get out and shut the door and slide open the side
door and grab the carpet cleaner. I wonder if the
thing even works. The cord is wound tightly around
the handle and tucked through the coil like a noose.

"What're you bringing?" I say.

"Me? Screwdriver."

"You sure?"

"Shit, meh. If I can't fix it with a screwdriver,
nobody can fix it." He chuckles his mischievous
chuckle. Fernando always pronounces "screwdriver"
with at least five syllables. Nervous as I am, I have to

grin.

I lift the carpet cleaner out and let it clunk onto the pavement. Fernando's work phone rings. He flips it open and puts it to his ear.

"Yo." He holds up a finger for me to wait, and I lean there on the carpet cleaner. The street is empty. No one in the windows. A few moments later, Fern's head is shaking.

"Man, you gotta be kidding me. We just got here. I told you you shouldn't have sent him out alone. Yeah, we're in the middle of a job right now... Yes... Alright... Sure, I'll let you know... Alright, bye." He snaps the phone shut and drops it in his pocket. He looks pissed.

"What is it?"

"Your buddy Alex went out by himself and made a mess. We gotta help post-job."

Alex isn't my buddy, that's just how Fernando makes it clear that someone isn't *his* buddy. He's always *your* buddy.

"What happened?"

"I dunno meh. You don't have his number, do you? The message came into dispatch through the system."

"Alex won't use his phone for work. Nobody has his number. Where is he?"

"Orange Oaks, about forty-five minutes. I told her we're in the middle of something. If we stall, maybe she'll send someone else." He sighs. "Dammit, Isabella's gonna be pissed if I'm late for love night, meh. *Pissed.*"

Fernando had explained to me several times that Wednesday was his and his wife's "love night." That's what he calls it anyway. And in case you're wondering, yes, it's exactly what it sounds like. Corny as it sounds, there's also something enviable about Fernando's little mid-week holiday. My wife doesn't even look at me unless she has to. If it weren't for the kids, I'm pretty sure she wouldn't have anything to do with me at all.

He flips his famous screwdriver the way he does, the flat head flashing in the sunlight, and tucks it in his belt. He could've been a bartender. "Alright, let's go. Got the glove?"

"Yeah, got it."

"Okay, let's do this fast. Maybe we can hurry up

and get back on schedule."

I'm always in awe of Fernando's apparent comfort before a job. Never any sign of nerves. The same goofy, wobbly walk, side to side, on his thin-soled sneakers. We approach the door. I put the heavy machine down and ring the bell.

"She always gives me shit when I'm late on Wednesday. I tell her there's nothing I can do about it, but she doesn't care. Then I gotta hear it—"

The door opens.

There he is, Harold Chapman. Big guy, maybe six-foot-four. Maybe two-hundred-fifty pounds. A big boy.

"Mister Chapman, how are you this morning?" says Fernando.

"Thank you for coming on such short notice. This stain is just an eyesore." He pulls the door all the way open and steps back. Fern grins at me, he knows exactly what I'm thinking. And yes, I'm glad I passed on leading this one.

"No problem at all, I understand, sir."

Mr. Chapman motions for us to come on in. Fernando goes in first, and I follow, yanking the carpet cleaner over the doorsill. Chapman winces, as though I might damage the fine piece of woodwork by doing so. I notice Fernando eyeballing our surroundings as we enter.

Methodology, principle #20:
Awareness of surroundings

"The spill is in the living room. Right over here." Chapman leads us to the stain, a darker, browner one than I'd expect from wine.

"Can you believe what the cunt did to my rug?" he says. "A thirty-year-old bottle of Chianti. I don't know what I was thinking when I married her." He turned to face us, his cheeks mottled red. "So can you get rid of it?"

I take my glove out of my pocket and put it on. Chapman watches me queerly for a moment, but returns his look to Fernando.

"Oh yeah, I can clean it, no problem. And uh...hey, is that an expensive shirt?"

All Chapman has on is a white undershirt, but he glances down to check anyway. That's all the time it

takes. Fernando plants his heel, pulls the
screwdriver, and lunges on his right leg. He wields
the tool like a tiny fencing sword. And with only the
minimum effort necessary, he pushes the
screwdriver into Mr. Chapman's eyeball.

Methodology, principle #1:
Technique, Technique, Technique

"The eyes are the windows to the soul," they say.
But to "poppers" like Fernando, the eyes are just a
fast track to the frontal lobe.

Mr. Chapman doesn't scream—they never do. It's
that short moment of preposterous confusion that
allows us to subdue him quietly. The mail-gloved left
hand goes over Mr. Chapman's mouth, my left instep
on his calf, and my right arm around his neck. The
first time I'd attempted this maneuver, I didn't
position my foot properly on the calf, and the man
came down backwards on top of me. Fortunately, he
was half the size of Mr. Chapman here. This time,
technique is crucial. *Technique, technique,*
technique.

I bend the knee, maintaining my center of gravity, and Fernando scoops out the right leg with his ankle. His arms flail, instinctively reaching to cushion his fall. This is key. We get him down expertly—very gently for a man of Chapman's size, and Fernando straddles him with his knees pinning the upper arms, and turns his attention to the screwdriver again.

"Theeere we go, yooou're okay, bro," he says to Mr. Chapman as he thumps in the screwdriver with the heel of his hand. He always offers the subjects this kind of consolation. It isn't part of methodology; he's just trying to be pleasant about it. With a good, last thump, the screwdriver breaks through the eye socket and sinks to the hilt.

Fernando had done it so fast, Chapman hadn't even had time to protest. "See how I'm using the eye socket for leverage, meh?" I nod. "Round and round. You're okay, buddy, aaalmost done."

The stainless steel flathead screwdriver is Fernando's favorite tool, which he grinds and polishes extra-sharp at the tip. It's a round-barreled screwdriver, so he can smoothly work the shaft around the circular rim of the eye socket. The edges of a square-barreled screwdriver grind on the bone, and tend to shred the eyelids, he'd explained to me, and cause undue blood spillage.

Methodology, principle #11:
Avoidance of messes before they happen

Fernando churns the brains. Mr. Chapman wiggles his arms and legs, but these are involuntary reflexes; no threat to either of us. Satisfied that the brain is sufficiently disorganized, I remove my glove from over Mr. Chapman's mouth.

Methodology, principle #9:
Proper safety precautions

It isn't long before all movement stops. Mr. Chapman is quite sufficiently dead. The next step is to ensure we've made no mess, and if we have, to clean it up.

"Hold that steady, bro."

I hold the screwdriver in place while Fernando tilts

Mr. Chapman to check if he had urinated. If he had, he'd quickly remove the pants to keep from messing the carpet. If he hadn't, he wasn't going to urinate anytime soon. He obviously hadn't shit his pants. When they do that, it's obvious right away. To Fernando, this is the most distasteful part of the job.

"Did he make a pee pee?" I ask.

"Nah, looks good. Hold that steady."

A lifeless human head is more unwieldy than you'd think, particularly a big one. If I let it go, it will tilt over and spill its liquefied contents onto the rug. I've only made this mistake once, and the result was unpleasant enough to teach me my lesson.

Fernando's phone rings again and he gets goofily to his feet. "Just hold him steady for a minute meh, don't spill that."

"I got it."

Fernando frowns at the phone and holds it to his ear like it's something filthy. It's the office again.

"Yeah... Yeah, we're post-jobbing the Chapman place—hey, you know we have that stakeout later, right? We can't just drive all over New Jersey helping people out, meh."

He stands listening for a moment. I can hear the dispatcher's cool, reasonable tone in the receiver. Fern covers the microphone and tells me: "Bro, I don't know what your buddy did, but they want us to break off right away and go help him."

"You mean leave this here?" I said, but he was listening to the dispatcher again, with a finger in his other ear.

I look down at the body of Mr. Chapman next to his wine stain. If he'd only known why his wife *really* spilled that Chianti on the carpet. Soon, she'd have enough money to buy all the old Chianti she wanted. And at the end of the day, Fern will be able to afford a nice bottle for love night. Me, I'll have plenty for my six pack.

Chapman will have no trouble waiting for us to get back and post-job, but the idea of leaving a body behind on a tier-one is highly off-the-book; the same as an unfinished job. An act of neglect subject to discipline. Even discharge.

Fernando is pacing through the living room now. I'm no veteran of PHA, but I've been there long enough to know what this conversation is about without hearing both sides of it. Fernando, the dispatcher, and Alex are all trying to cover their asses.

Claire, back at the office, needs us to break off and help Alex immediately, but doesn't want to say it outright, because she'd be advising us to work against principle 19.

Methodology, principle #19:
No job left uncompleted

Fernando knows that, and has no problem disregarding principle 19, as long as it's by way of the greater principle 4.

Methodology, principle #4:
Work as directed

As far as Alex goes, he's in some serious predicament, and likely at fault for it. He put up a big, red flag, but sent it in through the system without telling Claire exactly what's wrong. Claire knows this, and stands to be blamed for not handling the situation properly if things go south. Claire also knows that Alex is being quiet because a little help might alleviate the whole situation, and no reports will need to be filed, and nobody will in trouble. But for all of this to go smoothly, at least one of them has to put their ass on the line, and it's not going to be Fernando.

"I'll break off Claire, but only if you tell me to, bro. I'm not going unless you're officially directing me to. So what do you want me to do?" He rolls his eyes at me. My arms are getting tired. Mr. Chapman has a head like a watermelon. I can feel the stew sloshing around in his skull.

"Thank you. See, was that hard? Don't worry, I'll leave matches on the mailbox, yes... Yes... Alright, I'll let you know. Okay, bye."

He closes the phone and puts it in his pocket. From his other pocket he produces a book of matches and kneels down and puts it in Chapman's pocket. He doesn't say anything. I can tell he's annoyed.

"So much for principle 19," I say.

"I know, meh."

Fernando paces around annoyedly for a moment.

25

"Oh, did you see how I pushed with my back foot? From the heel of the back foot. You see why I like sneakers?"

"Yeah, I saw."

"Good."

I hold Chapman's head steady while Fern grabs a roll of black tape and a rag, and we pack the rag into his emptied eye socket and rip lengths from the roll of tape and paste them over his eye, sealing it shut. Still, I take two brass bookends from a nearby shelf and set each one against each ear. They should keep his head nice and straight until we get back, but the rag and tape will prevent a leak if they don't.

"Ok, meh, let's go see what's going on with your buddy."

He seems to be lightening up already. I'm glad for that.

On the way out, Fern drops a matchbook on the front stoop, and kicks it over so the PHA letters are visible. Then we get in the truck and punch the address for Alex's job in the GPS and leave. The way things are going so far, love night is far from certain.

2

WE'RE MOSTLY QUIET on the way to Orange Oaks, dreading the mess that awaits us at Alex's job. The adrenaline from the Chapman job had run its course, and now I'm tired again. I've been sleeping terribly lately. Most nights I just pass out on the couch. Ashley watches her shows in the bedroom, and I sit drinking my beer in the living room. Sometimes I watch TV, sometimes I read magazines. Last night, I just kind of sat there. That's just the way things are right now.

Fernando has been rubbing his bald scalp.

"Check this out, meh." Keeping his eyes on the road, he tilts his head to show me a fresh scab on top, about the size of a quarter.

"Ouch. What happened?"

"Dude, I was hammering some nails sticking up out of the floorboards back down, and of course, Angelica wants to help me. So I'm down there and she's helping with this little ball peen hammer I had from somewhere, and she goes, 'Daddy, I'm Handy Manny!' Some cartoon she likes. Anyway, the hammer hits me before I can even look up. I see stars, I go down. I don't know how long I was out. I get up, and get this—she's watching Handy Manny."

"You were knocked out?"

"Out cold, meh. I swear these kids are trying to kill me sometimes. I still have a scar from that paint stripper."

"I remember that one."

"I wish I didn't, meh. And remember this?" He lifts up his pant leg to show the hairless mound of scar tissue. "With the broomstick in the spokes? That one knocked me out too, meh."

"Jesus, how many times have you been knocked

28

unconscious?"

"A dozen, maybe. But like ten from the kids."

"What is the saying—how sharper than a serpent's tooth it is to have a thankless child?"

Fern looks sideways at me.

"You and your quotes, meh."

English is Fernando's second language—sometimes it takes him a second to work out a sentence with unusual syntax.

"Shit, meh," says Fern. "I don't think they're thankless, I just think they're trying to kill me!"

The GPS tells us our destination is on the left. As we pull up in front of the house, I see Alex's truck backed into the driveway, the bulkhead door wide open. He must be in there. If he isn't, he's blatantly disregarding principle 18, an act subject to discipline.

Methodology, principle #18:
Vehicle security

Fernando parks the truck and we get out and approach the vehicle. I knock gently on the hood, and Alex's head pops up in the cargo area. He must've been cooping back there for awhile. Not a good sign.

He slides the door open and invites us in. Even in the dark of his new uniform clothes, you can see he's soaked in sweat and blood.

"Jesus, I'm glad to see you guys." There's blood in the whiskers of his chin. He'd been struck in the lip.

"What's the matter, meh?"

"He just kept coming. I couldn't get him down."

"You didn't butterfinger it, did you?" I say.

"No, he didn't get away. He's dead, but Jesus. Head like a...I don't even know."

Alex was exhibiting all the symptoms of what PHA techs call "blood fever." A major-league freak-out after a messy job. This is forgivable; there isn't a technician I know of that is innocent of freak-outs— even Fernando had lost it a few times in his fledgling years. We all have stress-related dreams about work too; it's something about burning nasty chemical images in the brain with adrenaline as a kind of catalyst. Or at least that's how it was explained to me. Just shop-talk, really.

My own dreams are the nervous type. A recurring nightmare of mine is driving all the way back to headquarters and realizing I'd forgotten to pick up a body. Another is that I'd taken a nap and slept right through my lunch break. In these dreams, I'll wake up past sundown with a full barrel in the back and two incomplete jobs. The dreams diminish as time goes by, but I still have one or two a week. And Fernando is never in them. In my nightmares, I'm always alone.

"Sounds like you got a mess in there, meh."

"God, yeah. You guys have a carpet cleaner, right?"

"Yeah, we got one."

"Thank Christ."

"What did you use?" Fernando asks him.

Alex's silence was telling. After a long moment came the admission. "A Louisville Slugger," he says.

"The customer *requested* it?" suggests Fern. Occasionally the customer wants to choose the manner of death, and a technician is selected according to their personal preference. Luckily, these kinds of thematic requests are rare. All three of us know the truth—that Alex had been careless. Fern is just busting balls.

"Nah, I just... It usually works fine, you know? One, maybe two lumps."

Alex is a three-year guy, not green, but certainly not beyond a mistake. A baseball bat is a careless and unprofessional way to perform a job, and it's clear he'd gotten too cocky in his limited experience. It's better to be overly careful than cocky and reckless. To use the *right tool* for the job. That's a principle.

Methodology, principle #35:
Proper tools for the appropriate applications

This is never a baseball bat. The senior techs say it best: a baseball bat is for baseball.

Alex is a known basher, meaning he likes to do his jobs with blunt objects. The advantage of bashing is the decreased need for accuracy, but the drawback is the potential for a big mess. And a bat is a terrible instrument to bash with; everything from lack of concealability to the extra space it takes to wield it. After this is over, he'll have to seriously rethink his methods. Unless there *is* no *after this*.

"Maaan, what the hell you using a bat for? Don't you have a crackjack in here?"

"Yeah, It was dumb, I know it, I just kind of... It's a bad habit."

Fernando shakes his head and peeks out the windshield for unwanted attention.

Methodology, principle #20:
Awareness of surroundings

Nobody anywhere.

"Alright, let's have a look," Fernando says.

"I'll grab the cleaner," I say.

We walk up the stairs to the porch, and you can smell the blood before we even get to the screen door. "Bro, you gotta be kidding me," says Fernando. He opens the door, and I take a deep breath of fresh air before I go in.

Inside, it looks like the set of a slasher film. Smears on the tile floor, spatter on the walls. Bloody footprints on the carpet beyond the kitchen, both the victim's and Alex's. A bloody handprint on the calendar hung on the refrigerator door, as though marking down some special occasion. Alex looks ashamed, like a kid who's just broken a window.

"Bro, this is amateur shit right here, meh."

"I know. I know it."

Out in the dining room, a table is collapsed on splayed legs. A red, stucco mess down the middle. Broken dishes. A bloodied tablecloth bunched up on the floor. Glops of aborted matter all over the carpet. A strangeness suddenly comes over me as I realize how much of the man I'm seeing before I see the man himself. Sometimes it's these little oddities that leave the biggest impressions on me. At times I find myself thinking: *you know, this really is the strangest job.*

Last week, I took the family to the mall. Ashley and I and the kids were sitting in front of Orange Julius, and I was watching the two girls behind the counter make milkshakes and ice cream sundaes for a group of carefree teenagers. The twins were enjoying their ice cream, and I was thinking: *what a pleasant job those two young ladies have.*

I pictured that one of those girls marries some old,

rich guy; maybe a guy with a lot of money and not much else. She has an affair with the young, handsome pool boy, maybe realizes she made a big mistake marrying the old man after all. But that's alright, she can divorce the guy and make out like a bandit, right? Some long, ugly divorce proceedings later, Fernando and I find her name on our clipboard one morning. *Customer req. suffering. Pls bash. Picture conf. Thx.*

There are 43 work methods to follow as a technician of Pale Horse of the Apocalypse Inc. I kind of added my own unofficial principle number 44: leave work *at work*. It's easier said than done, but I do make it a point to try. Fernando says it becomes easier with experience. But I watched those girls pouring strawberry syrup over the ice cream, with those dark, wet chunks of strawberries, and no matter how hard I tried not to picture it, all I saw were those clots of gore that end up everywhere when you bash a guys's brains all over the place.

Simmons usually does those jobs. He's got these Mark McGuire arms. Uses a pipe bender.

The real strawberry sundae is in the living room. Back on Maple Street in Turnersville is a job murdered so neatly and professionally, it could've been filmed for a PHA instructional video. This one, however, was fit for a gag reel.

The scene is reminiscent of the big bang itself; a great explosion of organic material. Proper bashing kills have been likened to flipping a steak on a grill— one flip. That's one strike on one side, one on the other if needed. No more. Unless you've got one of those Simmons jobs, where you were *supposed* to make a great big mess.

The man, African-American, age indeterminable by his present condition, looks as though Alex had struck him two dozen times. One of our little rules— not acknowledged in methodology, for the sake of political correctness—is not to bash African-Americans. They are thought to have particularly durable heads. PHA does not condone or tolerate racial insensitivity, but after a number of blunders like this in the past, it's practically implied.

"You smeared this brother all over the house, meh!"

"I know it. Never again with the bat."

"Bro, you'll be lucky if there *is* an again."

"You don't think they'll fire him, do you?" I say.

Fernando shakes his head. "Dude, we'll do what we can, that's all I can tell you."

"It's an honest mistake, man," protests Alex.

"You honestly broke like ten work methods, bro. You got matches?"

"Yeah, yeah," says Alex, and reaches into his pocket.

"Throw one on the table there. No, you know what, put one on the mailbox." He stands, hands on hips, assessing the apocalyptic mess. "Put two on the mailbox, bro."

"Two?" Alex says.

"We're gonna be here awhile bro. And if they're gone before we're done, you're putting out another one."

"I'll do it," I say. Alex sighs, but offers no argument. He hands me two matchbooks.

"On the flag on the mailbox, meh," says Fernando. "If there is one. If not, just make it kinda visible."

"Alright," I say.

I walk nonchalantly to the mailbox, checking my surroundings. Checking for faces in windows, stopped cars, exhaust plumes, brake lights, etcetera.

Methodology, principle #20:
Awareness of surroundings

I open the matchbook and put it around the flag and close it, so the red "PHA" is easily visible. It holds there nicely. I can only imagine the feeling a cop would have, seeing one of these little red logos. I still get excited at the sight of a one-dollar bill on the ground, and we technicians make an above-average living. For a cop, it would be like finding a *five-thousand* dollar bill. Imagine that. Not too bad at all.

Methodology, principle #39:
Discretionary use of matchbooks

I slide open the door and gather all the stuff in the cargo area we might need, so I won't have to come out again for more before we're post-jobbed.

Methodology, principle #6:
The right way the first time

I roll the drum out the back of the vehicle and set it on its wheels and put in all the cleaning stuff and roll it up to the porch. I grab both handles and walk it carefully up the steps, maintaining the natural curve of my spine, and establishing firm footing with each step.

Methodology, principle #32:
Proper lifting and lowering guidelines

Inside, the guys had gotten most of the corpse on plastic. Fernando is spraying bloodbuster solution on the walls, and had set Alex to deal with all the particularly icky stuff—notably brains—and he's scratching bits of gore out of the carpet and into the properly indicated biohazard bags.

Methodology, principle #42:
Proper containerization equipment

While Fernando works on the walls, I fire up the carpet cleaner. I hear the clink of bone fragments sucking up the intake and catching on the filter. The sudsy water running pink up the hoses, sometimes gushing plain red. Its amazing sometimes to see how much liquid can come out of a person.

It's 1:30 by the time we're carrying the full barrel down the porch steps. Alex and I hoist it onto the back of the truck and slide it across the time-smoothed diamond plate. Fernando is barking at his wife on the phone in Spanish.

"Thanks again," says Alex.

"That's alright."

Fernando flips the phone closed and stuffs it in his pocket. Then he frowns and pulls it back out and dials again.

"You have much more to do today?" asks Alex.

"One more. In Newton."

Fernando is waddling down the driveway, phone at his ear, gesturing with his free hand the way he always does when he's worked up. I figure he's probably trying to get out of the Newton job.

"I'm thinking about switching to popping," says

Alex. "Fernando teach you how to do it?"

"I've only done backup," I say. "But yeah, he's teaching me."

Alex is staring at his boots, playing with the gravel. "You practice at home on anything?"

"Nah, my wife thinks I'm a warehouse manager. She'd start to wonder if I started stabbing dummy heads in the garage. And she's probably looking for an excuse to get rid of me anyway."

"That's right, I forgot you're married."

"Yeah."

Alex is one of those single guys you don't know whether to pity or envy for it. Either way, it's easy to hate them.

Fernando comes back, the phone closed in his hand.

"Alright, meh, you get to go home early and *we* get to go do more work."

"They're bringing me in?"

"Yeah, that's what they told me to tell you. Terry said to bring coffee on the way back."

"Am I in trouble?"

"I don't know. Light with cream and a sweet and

Geoff Sturtevant

low."

Alex doesn't answer, just walks dejectedly down the driveway. Walking it off. I'm rolling the carpet cleaner back to our truck when he comes back.

"They're gone," he says.

"What's gone?"

"The matchbooks. Both of them."

"Oh. No kidding."

"It's probably that damn carpet cleaner," says Fern. "The thing probably dimmed all the lights in the neighborhood. Someone called the cops."

"Did you tell them we matched out?" says Alex.

"I told them *you* flopped two books, but it needed to be done." He's wiping down his hairy arms with a shop towel. "It could've been worse, meh. And this was a tier-two job, so it's not a loss or anything. Fifteen-grand, at least."

His phone rings yet again. He frowns and answers it.

"Yeah, Claire... Yeeeah?"

Fern is smiling now. "Sure, that's a great idea, why didn't I think of that? Yes, ma'am, I'll tell him. Okay, bye." He hangs up.

"Okay, Alex, they're bringing you in, but first you gotta pick something up."

"Besides coffee?"

"Yeah, besides coffee."

Fern punches Chapman's address into Alex's GPS and tells him where we left the matchbooks, so he can grab them on the way out. With that, Alex is off to Maple Street in Turnersville. It's going to be awhile before poor Alex is back on the road again, and by that time, he should have very different sensibilities.

As we pull away from the house, though, something occurs to me.

"Fern?"

"Yeah, bro?"

"How the hell is Alex gonna get Chapman out of the house and into a barrel by himself?"

Fernando pauses, then wheezes laughter.

"He's a professional, meh. He'll figure it out!"

"Well, if he throws out his back, at least he'll have a couple months to rest it."

"At *least* a couple. Oh, that's funny, bro."

I picture the mammoth man laying next to his good

chianti stain. "Let's hope he puts those bookends back."

3

A DAY IN THE LIFE of a Pale Horse of the
Apocalypse Inc. technician—or as my coworkers like
to call it, another day in paradise—begins at 9:00
a.m. Each team, usually a veteran and an apprentice,
is given an agenda, which may include a combination
of killings, stakeouts, and\or assists, in what
dispatch estimates should amount to a suitable
workday. As you might've guessed, they're hardly
ever on the money. One day you might get back to
home base with three full barrels by early afternoon,

and the next, you might roll in at 9:00 p.m. with nothing but assists to show for it. If a predictable workday is important to you, a PHA technician is not your type of job.

Regular re-certifications are required, so it isn't unusual to be relegated to training rather than sent out on the road. You can expect to be sent to training three or four times a month. Or, for extended periods, if you've screwed something up, like Alex had. In this way, training doubles as a form of discipline.

Some of these training re-certifications include: Methodology, Biohazard and Disposal, Form and Formalities, Tools and Applications, and Practical Safety.

Methodology, if you haven't figured it out by now, is the set of principles by which we work. Each technician is expected to memorize all forty-three of them, their explanations included, and we're routinely quizzed at random. Most of us can rattle them off without a problem, but mastering the principles on a practical level requires years of repetition; putting them into practice and repeating them until they've become second-nature. Fernando is a good example of a technician whose instincts have been modeled around proper methodology. Whether he can recite them or not has no bearing on his work at this point—he just *knows* them.

Biohazard and disposal certification includes blood and body fluids safety, and canning. The cans, corn-based, sixty-gallon drums, are used for carrying back, transporting, and disposing of corpses. These drums are handled under strict guidelines during transportation, both back to the hub, and out to the incineration station. I've never been to the incineration station. Fernando has. He says the corn-based barrels and flesh burning smells like a cookout.

Form and Formalities is a brief certification, but changes the most often. Those matchbooks are the basis of our formal dealings with the law. They aren't discussed between police and agencies, only quietly redeemed for cash; five-thousand bucks apiece, and ten-thousand for the black ones. The potential for these payoffs is factored into the cost of the job, and paid for by the customer. Think of it as insurance.

47

The incentive to keep the system quiet, un-abused and effective is self-evident.

Practical Safety is another pretty easy one; bites, cuts, sprains and strains, etcetera. Safety precautions and equipment. Most of the veteran guys have bite scars; a man in his death-throes can bite like a pit bull. Fernando and I were in the last practical class together, and the trainer had borrowed him as a kind of visual aid. I knew he'd been bitten a couple times, but it turned out he had bite scars all over him. At least ten still visible. One on his forearm was from choking a chinless man. This was so long ago, he hadn't even started popping yet. He had a few on each leg from pinning attempts, and one on his shoulder from a sloppy maneuver he couldn't quite explain. This in itself was telling; if you can't explain what happened, your technique was likely improper. The point of this display?

Methodology, principle #1:
Technique, technique, technique

Interestingly, with all these methods and

principles, you'd think we have specific tools
training, but no, we don't. Tools and techniques
attain legitimacy through repeated successes. Tried
and true methods, like Fernando's screwdriver, or
Olivetti's choke, are both good examples. Every
technician has his own strengths and weaknesses,
and will adapt these successful tools and techniques
into what works best for him. Bad, loud, or
excessively destructive weapons are prohibited, but if
creative freedom is allowed anywhere at PHA, it is in
this area.

We walk into Fortissimo Restaurant at 3:15, more
or less on schedule. Fernando has on his plain red
cap, the one with the camera embedded in the brim.
He's in a fine mood now—looks like he's going to be
on time for love night after all.

This is a stakeout. Most of of the time, at least two
stakeouts are performed prior to a zone-three job—
(light commercial). This is also a tier-two job—
(subject to be left on-scene). Jobs like these are
prepared for carefully. By the time the technician
comes in for lunch, he'll have all the information he

needs, without ever having shown his face here prior.

The target is the proprietor, John Frizelli. The job has *mafia* written all over it.

Organized crime-related hits are out of alignment with our code of ethics, but the money for a zone-three, tier-two job is too much for our sales team not to feign ignorance. Tier-two, zone-threes almost always stink of organized crime. When somebody wants a body to be left in public, it is more often than not, to make a point.

The unspoken truth is, where highly professional jobs need to be carried out, PHA is the industry standard. Carrying out your own mob-related hits in this day and age is akin to filing your own tax returns. When there's a lot at stake, the obvious choice for anyone with money is PHA. So, ethical or not, we end up with our share of mob-jobs.

"Who'd you say has this one?" Fernando says.
"Olivetti."
"Big Olive, huh? I'll bet he grabs some lunch first."
"Well, we'll report on the food too."
The host leads us to a booth, and I sit facing the

door. Fern orders an antipasto appetizer. He shifts uncomfortably in his seat, and reaches down and pulls out his screwdriver and lays it on the table next to his silverware.

"Why'd you bring that?" I say.

He shrugs. "Principle two, bro."

Methodology, principle #2:
Preparedness (always be prepared)

"Fair enough. But could you put it somewhere else?"

"It's clean, meh."

"I know, it just doesn't belong on the table next to silverware, God, what's wrong with you, seriously."

"Alright, alright, I'll put it in my sock." He leans to the side and tucks the screwdriver in his black dress sock.

"Your table manners leave a lot to be desired, Fern. Frankly, you've got no business in a nice place like this."

He chuckles. "Eh, I'm just a country boy, gimme a break."

"A Costa Rican country boy?" I say.

"Yeah, bro. There's two kinds of us down there, meh, the country ones and the city ones. I'm from out in the country. We didn't even have electricity growing up, meh."

"Is that right?"

"Yeah, bro. Just candles."

"No TV?"

"You know a TV that runs on candles, meh?"

I grin. "So what did you do for entertainment?"

He has to think about this for a minute, then his face shows the recollection of a fond memory. "You known what we did? You tie tin cans together, then you tie them to a horse's tail, and then you slap the horse on the ass and it runs around like crazy. They're scared shitless while the cans clank around. Funny shit, meh. That's mostly what we did."

I let this sink in for a minute. "That's what you did for fun?"

"Yeah, meh. We always had tin cans. That's what you use to hold the candles up, meh."

A few minutes later, I'm sketching a rough layout

of the dining room in my notebook, and Fernando is looking around with his hat on, taking video footage. The waiter comes by with our appetizer and drinks, and we tell him to his visible dismay that that's all we'll be having today. We've got work to do.

The front door opens, and a gigantic, well-dressed figure enters. Gigantic, well-dressed, and visibly annoyed. The host approaches him while I watch. It isn't long before I realize whom I'm looking at.

"That's the guy there."

Fernando tilts a shiny butter knife on end and looks in the reflection behind him. If it were anyone but Fernando, I'd have told him: "don't look now, but..." But Fern is a pro.

"You sure, meh?"

I nod. I'd studied his pictures in the work order. There's no mistaking the profile alone. The back of his neck bulges with obscene bunches of fat. He makes Chapman look like a fitness model. A walrus of a man.

"He's a big boy," Fernando says, still gazing into the side of the knife.

Frizelli is chastising the host somehow. I put in my

earbud to listen along; a Bluetooth device attached to my recorder. I'm curious to hear what the hubbub is about. Fernando watches along in the reflection.

Can't you do anything by yourself? How am I supposed to trust you to keep this place running if you can't handle a fuckin' toilet?

I'm sorry, I tried the plunger. If it was a plunger thing, we wouldn't be having this conversation, believe me.

Ain't there anyone you can call for shit like this?

Well, yeah, but I thought you might wanna look at it before some gavone comes in here and charges us who-knows-how-much.

What are you, a fuckin' idiot?

No sir, I just...

What do I say about taking initiative?

You said to take initiative.

What did I say about it? Am I speaking fuckin' Chinese here?

No sir.

That it's the core of fuckin' management! If you can't take fuckin' initiative, how are you supposed to fuckin' manage?

I understand, sir. I will from now on, I promise. Lesson learned.

"He's fuckin' perturbed," I say.

"I can tell, meh."

I nod. "Said there's a problem with the bathroom or something."

I hand Fern the Bluetooth earbud. He listens amusedly and watches the exchange continue. After awhile, he sets the knife down.

"There's gonna be a problem, meh. Olivetti's a choker." Fernando has that look on his face; the gears grinding.

I nod in understanding. He doesn't mean Olivetti is the type to fold under pressure. He's referring to the way Olivetti kills his marks. Choking is one of the few bloodless kills on the menu, making him a popular choice for zone-three jobs, where post-jobbing needs to be done in a hurry. These jobs are usually performed in quiet, private areas— bathrooms are a good choice. Mercifully, Frizelli would be left on-scene. Moving a body that big is a lofty endeavor.

55

"All his kills are chokes," I say. "Hates blood."

Fern bends an eyebrow at me. "Can you picture choking that guy, meh?"

I look at Frizelli. I try picturing my legs around his midsection, a forearm clamped under his chin. Even in my imagination, I can't do it. As if Frizelli somehow senses my thoughts, he glances over. Quickly, I look down.

"You're right," I say.

"You can't choke out that guy. That's one big fucker right there, meh."

"They say Olive could strangle a bull."

Fernando chuckles. "He could, bro, I've seen him. The guy is good. But a bull has a neck."

We watch in the bar mirror as Frizelli walks to the back. The waiter comes by to check if we haven't changed our mind about ordering entrees. Fern tells him we're fine. He leaves, and Fern pulls out his phone.

"I'm calling Olive, meh."

"Here?"

"Just keep an eye out, meh."

I can hear Olivetti's phone ringing through the

receiver. I pop a bruschetta in my mouth.

"Olive. It's Fernando." He speaks quietly, checking constantly for anyone within earshot. No-one around; no patrons, no waiter.

"Like four-hundred pounds, bro... No shit. You can't do the guy man, seriously, it's not a good idea, he's got no neck or anything... Yeah, and if you end up under him... Yeah, if you want... I know, bro, I'll split it with you. Either way, bro. Okay."

This goes on for a minute before they have an agreement. Fernando hangs up.

"I'm gonna do him," Fern says. "We're splitting the check."

"Alright. When's it scheduled?"

Fernando bends an eyebrow at me.

"Hold on," I say. "You mean now?"

"Methodology principle 26, bro."

Methodology, principle #26:
Don't hesitate, trust your instincts

"Olive can't do this guy, bro. He needs to be popped."

He takes the screwdriver and slides it back under his belt. And there goes my heart. So much for an easy stakeout.

"You're crazy, Fern. Jesus."

Frizelli's ass is sticking out of the stall when we enter the men's room.

"Shitter's out of order," Frizelli says, hearing our footsteps. "The pisser's fine."

Fernando waddles ahead of me and motions for me to stand at the urinal. I face the wall and pretend to use it. Fern knocks on the partition, and Frizelli steps backwards out of the stall.

"You gentlemen alright?"

"Yeah, sorry, I didn't mean to bother you, sir. Just wanted to ask, are you happy with your current wine distributor?"

Frizelli looks tentatively relieved, then annoyed. "Believe me, chico, you couldn't compete with my distributor. You delivery guys?"

I have that feeling in my thighs, that sour weakness. I can hear my own heartbeat. Everything looks sharper, has a tinge of blue, and I see my reflection in the chrome of the urinal's flush lever. Behind me, the black of an enormous suit jacket.

"Well, we *are* offering a free case to any new potential clients today. Today only." Fernando's voice shows no sign of stress. For the life of me, I don't know how the hell he does it. And me, why the hell am *I* doing this? I'm supposed to be a novelist. A professor. Something...

"Oh yeah?" Frizelli smooths down his lapels and steps forward. "What kind of vino we talking here?"

Fernando has his eye on Frizelli's shirt. "Bummer about that stain, meh." Frizelli glances down. That's my cue. There will be no second chance to do this right.

I turn from the urinal and jump on Frizelli's calf and swing my arm around his neck just as Fern lunges in. In one smooth motion, I grab the bicep of my other arm and squeeze. All at once, I understand why Fernando had deemed this man unchokeable. He doesn't budge at all under my weight; it's like hanging onto a brick wall. If he were to get his hands on me, I'd be helpless.

Right on schedule, Frizelli's head bounds

backwards, and I know Fernando has struck, *thank God.*

But something is wrong.

Fernando's shoe had squeaked on the tile floor. I'd heard it. He'd slipped.

"Shit," says Fernando, and just like that, Frizelli bucks me off his back like an angry bull. I bounce against the partition and land on my feet, but I'm disoriented, and I nearly slip myself. Frizelli stumbles and lands with his back in the urinal, snapping wall tiles like crackers. Somewhere, the screwdriver clanks to the floor. Fernando is scrambling to hone in on it.

Suddenly, I meet eyes with Frizelli. An attitude of murder where there'd normally be astonishment. Not astonished at all. In a glance, I know he'd been half-expecting this. Above his eyebrow, an obscene tear in the flesh of his forehead. Fern had missed his mark.

It happens in a literal heartbeat. The skin splits wide, shrinking back over the bone. For a moment, you're not sure if it's going to bleed at all. Then, all at once, ribbons of blood. Before you know it, it seems like gallons of it are everywhere. The eyebrows, for reasons unknown, are direct portals to the circulatory system.

All this had taken place in under two seconds, but the irony of Fernando slipping in his thin-soled sneakers had occurred to us both immediately. And things are about to get even more slippery.

"You dead fuck!" says Frizelli, reaching into his jacket. I bolt for the stall, my body electric with adrenaline, bracing for the gunshot I knew was coming.

But here comes Fern. He butterfly-smacks Frizelli's wrist, sending the gun skittering across the floor. It careens off the wall and under the partition, knocking the lost screwdriver into view. I pick it up. There's a bit of flesh still dangling from the blade.

"You filthy prick!" Frizelli swings a fist. Fern parries, nearly slips again. Blood is pouring in buckets, and his sneakers are slick with it. But here I come, sneaking up behind Frizelli in my non-slip boots, my instincts taking over. Fern's drills play in my mind, his work on the dummies back at the hub. *You don't have to hit hard, meh. Just connect. Let the screwdriver do the work.*

Thinking too much is what always fucks me up. Stabbing someone in the brain through the eye isn't unlike connecting with a golf ball or throwing a dart. You don't want to think about it too much, just focus on the target and make contact.

Heels planted, I bring the screwdriver around Frizelli's giant head and plug it in. The blade connects with the rear of the socket. One light out. He spins to face me.

Fern wastes no time—he's on his back like a monkey. Frizelli reaches up and grabs hold of Fernando's left ear. Fern yelps but doesn't let go. He grabs a handful of Frizelli's jacket and steps on the back of his leg. An audible snap, and Frizelli is forced to take a knee. Fern stretches the fabric across his mouth and nose.

"God damn! Kick the balls bro! Kick balls!"

I wind up and drive my boot into Frizelli's crotch. And again. Muffled moans from under the fabric. He lets go of Fernando's ear. Fernando arches his back and forces him backwards. They crash down, tile cracking. Fern is sitting behind him, choking him with his own collar, knees against his shoulders for leverage. Frizelli's face is turning purple.

Just like that, I've taken the lead. I straddle Frizelli and pound the heel of the screwdriver until it sinks to the hilt. Then I stir, chipping away the thin bone of the eye socket. He vibrates, his circuits firing random impulses. Soon the resistance eases, a sensation like a fork in a bowl of jello. I keep stirring. My forearm burns with the acid of exertion. I realize I'm grinding my teeth.

Eventually, he is still.

Fernando lets go of the jacket and gets to his feet. He rubs his ear.

"Good job, meh. God damn..."

I'm too wound up to answer. I feel a little like my own brains have been stirred.

"This one's 30/70, meh."

"Thanks. You alright?"

"Yeah bro." He pulls his screwdriver out and kicks Frizelli's head sideways. Clots of brain dribble out onto the floor. A grimace frozen on Frizelli's mouth. A picture is worth a thousand words. That wasn't aways a cliche, mind you. It used to be Confucius.

I survey my condition, as we've been trained to do after a disagreeable job. We'd both managed to stay surprisingly clean, considering the mess. Fern's hairy forearms are smeared from the struggle, but he has on short sleeves, and can wash them off in the sink. I have blood on my hands and the seat of my pants, but that's no big deal either. Considering the cataclysmic condition of the bathroom, we manage to walk back into the dining room looking relatively professional. They're going to have to find someone else to fix that toilet.

Methodology, principle #32:
Proper form and formalities

Fifteen minutes later, Fernando and I are sitting at the table, eating the rest of the bruschetta. Fern sips his mint tea, reading a folded section of the paper he'd grabbed on the way out of the bathroom. He'd texted Olivetti: *All done. Tell you about it later. Waiting for the cops.* A smile comes across his face, exposing the silver lining of his veneers.

"Fuckin Hagar, bro. I used to love this one. Here,

check it out." He turns the paper around so I can read it.

Helga, Hagar's wife, is waiting at home for him to return from work. For the wife of a Viking, a violent, thieving killer, Helga is pretty easygoing, turning a blind eye to her husband's wicked ways, and waiting patiently for him to return, so that they and their daughter can enjoy some semblance of a family life.

Hagar comes home drunk again, having spent a night at the pub, undoubtedly attempting to sterilize his soiled conscience with alcohol. Perhaps he's unable to face his family, hoping they'll be asleep by the time he got back. But Helga is fed up with Hagar's nonsense. She'd had it *up to here*.

Helga says something to Hagar, and he says something back—I never get the chance to read the real dialogue; the speech bubbles seem empty to me. Maybe Hagar needs to shape up or ship out; she's sick of his reprobate behavior. But reprobate behavior was Hagar's *job*. He was only trying to forget it. Maybe drinking the way he did was the only way to adhere to principle 44; to leave work *at work*.

Fern is expecting a chuckle, but I'm lost in my

imagination at the moment. Because it occurs to me suddenly how similar—

All at once, red and blue lights wash over the bar. The police. Fernando watches through the mirrors and pops an antipasto in his mouth and sits back and wipes his hands on the cloth napkin.

"Just look down, meh. Just listen." I nod, and flip to another page of the paper.

Two policemen enter, and the manager hurries over and gestures exasperatedly, motioning to the bathroom. The cops look about, and I look down at the paper. Fernando lifts his arm and rubs the top of his bald head. The high is ninety degrees today, I read. Eighty-four tomorrow. I don't look up. I don't need to. I can *feel* the cops looking at us.

More lights, and the door opens, but I keep my eyes on the paper. The employees are whispering hurriedly. The sound of sturdy boots moving to the back of the restaurant. The manager's nervous scurries here and there. Slower steps now, two sets of heavy boots approaching the table. Fernando and I couldn't appear more ignorant, just enjoying a leisurely afternoon.

"Afternoon, folks," one cop says, a young rookie, his voice a fabricated baritone. The other officer seems much more comfortable, an older fellow with a grey mustache. Comfortable, until a vague look of recognition shows in his eyes.

"Afternoon, officer," says Fernando, with too many syllables. He peeks outside, pretending to notice the lights for the first time. "Did I park illegally, sir?"

"No, sir, there's been an incident. We're going to need to bring you down to the station for some questioning."

"Questioning? Feel free to join us here." Fernando pushes out a chair and motions for them to sit down. The young cop shakes his head and opens his mouth to speak. Fernando interrupts him: "Are we in any kind of danger?"

"Not now sir, no danger at all, but I'm afraid I must insist you—"

The older cop steps in, his hand on the young man's back. "Gentlemen, have you noticed anything out of the ordinary here this afternoon?"

Fernando looks at me. I shrug, and he looks back at the officer. "No, nothing unusual. Besides this unusually delicious antipasto appetizer." He offers some to the cops. The young one holds up his palms. The older one allows a smile.

"Any...evidence, perhaps? Anything we ought to have a look at?" The young cop looks quizzically at his partner, as if he were witnessing some police procedure he missed at the academy.

"Now that you mention it," says Fernando, "you know what? I found these on the table." He takes two PHA matchbooks out of his breast pocket and puts them on the table. The cop widens his eyes at them, then picks them up and puts them in his pocket.

"Thank you, I'll submit these for evidence."

"Glad to help."

"You two ought to hurry along," the officer says. "to make way for the detectives."

"I would hate to get in the way. Come on, meh."

"Let's have you go out the side door there, heh? Don't worry about the check."

More cherries light up the mirror behind the bar. It's about to get pretty busy in here.

"No problema. Let's go, bro."

4

WE'RE OVER THE COUNTY LINE by 4:30, on pace to punch out before 5:30. Not only had we gotten all our work done, but someone else's botched job as well. Fernando was happy because he'd have no trouble getting home on time for love-night, and I'm a bit enamored with myself for my first successful pop-job. On a true bad-guy, no less. I almost hate to admit it, but I'm proud of myself. I wasn't supposed to be a technician, you know. I was supposed to be a novelist. Maybe a professor. Something like that.

Fernando's phone rings a little way down the highway. He looks at the number and frowns, which means it must be the office.

"Yeah... What? Oh hell no! You know Wednesdays are bad, bro... Oh yeah? How are you gonna make it worth my while?" He sits listening quietly for a minute.

My mind is still back at Fortissimo. You know, the more I think about it, the most distasteful part of that job wasn't what you'd think. It wasn't the violence, it wasn't the blood—I'd seen bathtubs-full of blood today—It was that fresh-faced, brand-new cop, set out to uproot and destroy evil, having his world turned upside-down. Everything he thought was sacred, tossed to the dogs. The realization that right and wrong don't matter nearly as much as he thought they did. I'm sure he's sitting quietly in the passenger seat of his cruiser right now, thinking back to Ethics 101, struggling to pair what just took place with the philosophies of Immanuel Kant. Of Aristotle. Of Friedrich Nietzsche. Everyone has to lose their innocence eventually, I suppose. Observe, officer, there are no oysters. There are no pearls. But what red-blooded, American man, ethical or not, millennial or not, can't find a pearl in a pile of *five-thousand* clams? Distasteful, yes, no argument there. But by my age, most people would wipe their ass with an entire Ethics 101 textbook before they soiled a single dollar.

"Dude, are you serious?" Fernando is still on the phone with the office.

"What is it?" I ask. He doesn't answer me.

"Bro, you gotta be kidding me..."

"What is it?" I ask again. He glances at me a moment, but he's still listening.

"Yes, I know principle 31, bro, but I..."

Principle 31 is an important one; one of the few principles you could be *fired* for not following.

Methodology, principle #31:
Work as directed.

Not following this principle is insubordination. Obviously, they're pinning another job on us. Fern looks pissed, but the fight has gone out of him.

I take out my own phone and sit there looking at it. There'll be no love night at my house either way, but we normally get out pretty early on Wednesdays, and I watch the kids while Ashley goes out doing who-knows-what. I ought to call her and let her know I may be home a little later than usual.

I should, but I don't. I just don't care.

"A half-day, every Wednesday for a month, that's what I want," says Fernando.

"For doing one more job today?" I ask, but Fernando gestures at me to be quiet. I look down at my phone. It occurs to me that a month's-worth of early Wednesdays means a month's-worth of Wednesdays that I'll be home early. Home with the girls, playing teatime and princesses and dress-up. And Ashley will be there, silent and sullen. The underlying truth always resonating in the walls. It's not hate, it's worse; more like *nothing* than hate. Like a vacuum. You can't talk in a vacuum, you can't hear in a vacuum. You can't *breathe* in a vacuum.

There was a time in my life I would've been excited for a half-day in the middle of the work week—hump day, right, fellas? But now, I don't want to go home.

The truth—and I know how it sounds—is that part of me never wants to go home again.

Fernando swings onto exit 12, jarring me from my thoughts. "Sorry, I was daydreaming," I say.

"That's alright, meh."

"What's wrong? You sound a little forlorn all of a sudden."

He doesn't answer. I decide not to pry.

"So what are we doing?" I ask.

"Last minute job."

"Fast one?"

"Yeah. It'll be quick. I promise."

"No hurry for me. There's no love night in my house, Fern. No love *lost* in my house."

"Yeah, I know, meh."

We're quiet for awhile, headed west on the service road. Quiet road.

"Why you never tried love night, meh? I've been telling about it forever."

I snort at that. "Forever? I've only known you for eight months. And Ashley and I were way past the point of no return by then."

"That's a shame, meh."

"It's the life of Hagar, ya know?"

"Is that another one of your quotes?"

"Nah, the comic. Like the one you showed me at Fortissimo."

"Like Hagar? How's that, meh?"

"You know. The guy's out plundering and pillaging. Doing ugly stuff all day. And he just can't manage principle 44."

"Principle 44?"

"Yeah, remember? That's kind of my own principle."

"Oh, right. Don't bring the work home with you."

"I try not to."

The late-day air is cooler now, providing some relief. Still, the day's sweat just dries on you, leaving you sticky. The trees are thick along the service road. I smack a mosquito that lands on my arm.

"I think I'm pretty good at it," I say. "But I don't think it matters much. These days I just try not to bring home to work."

Fernando regards me with either condescension or sympathy, I can't tell which. And like principle 44, I don't suppose it makes a difference.

"But Hagar still cares, meh. I don't know how hard he tries, but he still cares."

"I dunno. You think so?"

"Yeah, bro. I wouldn't laugh if he didn't. There's nothing funny about that."

We were quiet for awhile while he drove. I took out my phone again and looked at it and scrolled to Ashley's icon. The picture is the same one I've had since the beginning. I remember taking it; the two of us at the Olive Garden. That was an extravagant dinner for us back then, we had no money.

No money, but we had something else.

What was so different now anyway? What had been so different for such a long time? Why did we let it happen? I've told myself time and time again that it just happens, but does it *really?* Or is it a cop-out? It hadn't happened to Fernando and his wife.

Is it possible for Ashley and me to get to a point again where we could have our own love night? I mean, we'd never call it that, that's too corny, but maybe date night? We can afford a babysitter now. We could even afford a truly extravagant dinner. We could, but maybe I'd just start by taking her back to the Olive Garden. Maybe that's what we could do. Try starting over again.

My thumb hovers over Ashley's icon. It hovers there, then withdraws. I shut off the screen and put the phone down on my thigh and hold it there a minute. Then I put it back in my pocket. Maybe tomorrow. Maybe tomorrow I'll try caring. That's always the best time to turn over a new leaf, isn't it—tomorrow.

"You think it's even fixable?" I ask Fern.

He sighs. "You just run out of options the longer you go, meh. Eventually, I guess...maybe you just run out of options altogether."

"Yeah," I say.

We pull over in an old, wooded lot. The sun is behind the tree line now, and it's a relief. It's been a long, hot, blood-soaked Wednesday.

"You gotta take a leak or anything?" Fern says.

"Nah, I'm fine," I say. "Are we close?"

"Yeah."

Fernando stretches his arms overhead. "They gave

me a month's worth of Wednesdays off."

"Off? No kidding…"

I reconsider my idea. Wednesdays off. Maybe I could make a project out of it. Family day. I could talk a lot, even if don't want to. I could be thoughtful, say nice things. I wouldn't think about work. I'd tell Ashley she looked nice, even if I didn't think so. And the kids. I'd do stuff with the kids. But mostly, I'd try to focus on Ashley. I'd try to see her the way I used to. I'd *try*.

"I'm off Wednesdays too, then?" I ask hopefully.

"Yeah, you too, meh."

"Are they paying you?"

"One kill's worth a day."

"That's great, man."

"Yeah."

Quiet on the road. Only the faint white noise of the highway in the distance. The sweat is drying under my scratchy polyester clothes, and the residual blood on the seat of my pants feels tacky on the canvass jumpseat. The worn diamond plate floor of the old truck. Blue stuff rocking back and forth in the opaque plastic windshield washer tank. Old bolts rolling down the road one by one; each day, the things we take for granted slowly disintegrating. All guys like us really have is our families to come home to. The smell of dinner when we open the door. The adoring kids, so happy to see daddy come home again. That's why we do this in the first place, isn't it?

The realization hits me like a shock. Just like that, I understand. The folly of my ways has never been so completely obvious. Clear as day. It's me. I'm the asshole. This whole time, *I've* been the problem. I have to fix my marriage before it's too late. *God, by now, she probably wants me dead...*

"Fernando, I've been thinking..."

He's turned to face me now, his feet planted flat on the floor. His hands in his lap.

"Bro," he said.

"What?"

"That's some stain on your shirt..."

THE
ORGANIZATION

1

I know how this sounds, but there's an unspoken rule in the grocery delivery business to avoid getting into conversations with the elderly while you're on the clock. Your perishables are likely to spoil before you make it to your next delivery. I happen to enjoy talking to my elderly customers, but it's true, they talk me to death.

Speaking of death, my customers love to bring that up—the subject is a kind of novelty to them. It's their own little dirty joke they can spout with impunity. I say they deserve it. While we all try so hard to ignore the fact of our mortality, they've earned the right to remind us that we're all going to end up in the same place. See, my customers don't fear death. What they fear is that no one will listen to them anymore. So I listen. And God knows, they talk me to death.

Hyacinth, formerly of apartment 211, once told me she couldn't wait to die. "Take me now," she said, "I'm ready. Take me, and take these arthritis fingers." Then her eyes darted around, sure she'd chanted some deadly incantation.

"Stop it," I said. "You're not going to die."

Hyacinth died shortly afterward, but not that afternoon. That afternoon, I left her very much alive, with all her fruits and vegetables. She was a nice lady.

So there I was again, bringing the old-timers their groceries. I parked the van in my usual spot in front of the building, close enough to load my cart on the sidewalk, but with enough space behind me for an ambulance to pull in. Five hundred tenants in their seventies, eighties, and beyond meant plenty of ambulance visits.

I loaded up my cart and wheeled it in. The familiar warmth and smell of an old closet. Off the atrium there's a common room where the old folks gather to chat and listen to big band music on the record player. Often you'll hear laughter mixed in with the music. Thundering old voices, everyone talking over their hearing aids. I tried to sneak by on my way to the elevators, but if any of my regulars were in there, I was sure to get dragged in for a little small talk. Today, Charlie Vandergrift spotted me and waved me in to join the chat. I left my cart in the hall and went on in. Gotta keep this short, I thought. *No open-ended questions.*

"Hey Charlie," I said.

"Heya, son. How's life?"

"Is he your son?" said Beattie Smith, apartment 127, "I didn't know you had a son."

"He's not my son."

"Because I didn't think you had a son."

"He's the delivery man, Beattie."

She looked at me, squinting behind her glasses.

"Oh, right. I thought you were his son. I was thinking to myself, I never knew the grocery man

82

was Charlie's son."

"Nope," I said. "No relation."

"The doctor says I have to have surgery," Charlie said.

"Good heavens," Beattie said, "why didn't you tell me?"

"I did, Beattie. I got something in my neck. I can't swallow right."

"That's awful," I said.

"I have to melt my pills in water and it tastes terrible."

"Helen says I should take vitamins," Beattie said.

"I never took 'em. It's enough trouble with the pills. They taste terrible."

"That sounds awful," I said.

"I had to put my steak in the food processor machine with gravy."

"Helen says I should take vitamins, but I don't know. I've got blood sugar already, what if it does something?"

"Vitamins shouldn't affect your blood sugar," I said.

"Oh, I don't know."

"I told the doctor, I said why bother," Charlie said. "I'm gonna be dead soon anyway, why cut me into pieces? I have to cut my food into pieces, now me too? Hell..."

"You're not going to be dead soon," I said, "stop it."

"I don't mind. Let me die before anything else goes wrong."

"Helen says I should take vitamins, what do you think?"

"I never took 'em," said Charlie.

"I better get going," I said. "Nice talking to you two. Take it easy, Charlie, feel better."

"Have a nice life, son."

"Is he your son?"

I had two deliveries. Agnes Brown, apartment 315, has no legs, so I helped her put her groceries in the cabinets and refrigerator. Then she insisted I wait while she rummaged through her purse to look for four quarters.

"Buy yourself a cup of coffee," she said.

Henry Thompson, apartment 220, was too proud to ask for help, but he did make me listen to his usual war story again—with its latest revisions:

"We're all hunkered down in the barracks getting shelled to hell and back. Hell yeah, I was scared, not too proud to admit it. Lucky the Krauts weren't wasting their good stuff on us, and no major damage. Then the squad leader says let's get out there and let 'em know we're doing just fine. So I'm out there behind the sandbags with a grenade launcher at two in the morning. I don't know if we got any of 'em, but we didn't lose anyone either. Lost some sleep though. I'm still tired. I'll be dead soon anyway."

"Oh stop it," I said.

Henry, like all the others, had no real money or family for support. This place was a godsend for the dispossessed elderly, a place to live for next to nothing. Modest as the accommodations were; tiny studio units, kitchenette and bathroom, without such cheap housing, these folks could never afford the groceries I brought them every day.

It was only that afternoon, pushing my empty cart back to the elevator, I got my first inkling that something was strange about Colosseum Retirement Home.

I heard some stifled commotion, and turned to see

the door to room 209 was slightly ajar. Ms. Higgins's place. I thought about ignoring it. It could've been anything—Ms. Higgins might have been constipated for all I knew. But what if she needed help? I decided to take a look. I nudged the door and peeked inside.

"Hello? Everything alright?"

What I saw nearly stopped my heart.

It was Darien and Sam, the facilities and maintenance guys. In between them writhed Agatha Higgins. They'd gagged her and bound her feet and hands with duct tape. Sam had her hooked under the arms and Darien was struggling with her kicking feet.

"Jesus, what are you doing?"

All three of them turned their heads my way. Ms. Higgins squealed unintelligibly behind the gag.

"Uh...hey Kevin," said Darien.

"Put her down!"

"You don't understand," said Darien. "Dammit Sam, you leave the door open?"

"Whoops," Sam said.

"What is there to understand?" I said.

"Hff!" said Ms. Higgins. Sam shushed her.

"Listen, Kevin," Darien said, "This isn't what it looks like. So keep your hat on, and please...keep your voice down."

Sam bit a length of duct tape off a roll and put it over Ms. Higgins's gag. She wagged her head to avoid it, but the tape went on. "That's better," he said. "I told you to shush."

"Do you really need to do that?" I said.

"Of course," Darien said. "You think we just tie up nice old ladies for no reason?"

"You know us," said Sam.

I did know them, at least casually, and I'd always thought they were good guys. But this didn't look so good.

"This doesn't look so good," I said.

"You're right," said Darien. "Out of context, this doesn't look so good. I get it."

"What context?"

Darien sighed. He and Sam glanced knowingly at each other.

"So what, are we supposed to tell him?" said Sam.

"I don't think we have a choice," said Darien.

"Tell me what?"

"Listen, Kevin, could you please just check and make sure no one's in the hall?"

I looked at Ms. Higgins, who seemed to be running out of steam. Then I looked at Darien. What should I do, yell for help? Call the police? But it was the expression on his face; more phlegmatic than anything, that stopped me. I found myself backing towards the doorway and looking out into the hall. "No one there," I said.

"Good," Darien said. "Let's go. Stay quiet Kev, we'll discuss this in the office."

I walked alongside Sam and Darien with Ms. Higgins in tow. She'd given up struggling and just hung limp while they carried her.

"Does she need medical care?" I asked. Maybe stubborn old Ms. Higgins needed a trip to the doctor and didn't want to go. Maybe that's all it is. The maintenance boys are good guys, they wouldn't do something like this without a good reason for it. Would they?

"Medical care, nah. She's fit as a fiddle."

We stopped at the end of the hall by the trash chute.

"Get that for me, Kevin?"

"What, the trash chute?"

"Yeah, grab the door there, would you?"

So I pulled open the door. The sour odor of garbage wafted up from below. Before I could even consider what I was doing, they'd hoisted Ms. Higgins and tipped her headfirst into the chute. I couldn't believe what I was seeing. This must be a joke.

"Don't worry," said Darien. "We're not hurting her." And they pushed her through the door until only her wiggling feet were visible. Muffled moans of exasperation echoed in the tin chamber. She was writhing like a nightgowned larva. Sam gave the bottoms of her dirty slippers a final push and with a squeak, she disappeared down the chute.

"I know what you're thinking," Darien said.

I didn't even know what I was thinking. I couldn't even speak.

"We didn't just throw Ms. Higgins in the garbage. Anything over a hundred pounds trips the diverter."

"So what the hell just happened? Is Ms. Higgins alright?" We sat at a folding table in the first-floor maintenance room, Sam and Darien's dim, greasy little hideaway. Darien offered me a cigarette, and I took it. I didn't smoke often, but I needed something, and maybe a cigarette was it.

"Okay, so here's the deal," Darien said. "You understand the basic premise of this home, correct?"

I should, I'd been delivering groceries here for years—A publicly-funded home for the forsaken elderly; helpless men and women without money or family. Five hundred ultra-efficient units on five floors. A merciful social project.

"Sure, of course," I said.

"Alright, so how do you figure a place like this stays in operation? Electricity, water, taxes, insurance, salaries, etcetera."

"And maintenance," added Sam.

"Donations and subsidies?" I guessed.

"Really...how much value in dollars do you think America places on our tenants here?"

"I never thought about it."

Darien nodded. He lit my cigarette, then his.

Sam was leaning against a filing cabinet eating potato chips. "Nice guys like you give people way too much credit."

"The truth is," Darien said, "the government, the public...people don't much revere their elderly."

"They know what's right," Sam said, "but it's a lot easier to turn their heads."

"A lot cheaper too," added Darien.

"I guess," I said.

Darien sat back and took a long drag from his cigarette. A cloud was gathering around the bare light bulb overhead. "Here's what they say when no one's listening: They live longer and longer, they eat all the food, they run up the bills, they're a burden. That's how they justify themselves. But want to know the truth?"

I nodded.

"The truth is, they remind us of what we're all trying to ignore. Our mortality."

"It's human nature," Sam said. "It's easier just to pretend they don't exist."

"And cheaper."

"I get it," I said, "but I don't get it. Where are you going with this? Is she alright?"

"The money. Like I was saying, even a supposed

non-profit organization like this one needs to make money. Nobody's doing this for free, and nobody's paying for it out of the kindness of their hearts."

"And nobody's doing all the upkeep out of the kindness of their hearts either," Sam added.

I took a short drag on my cigarette and coughed.

Darien grinned. "Not a smoker, are you?"

"Just a little wound up from before."

"I can see that."

I took a little drag and managed not to cough. "I'm still not making the connection here."

"We think you ought to see it for yourself," Darien said. "Tomorrow night. Be here at 10:00 pm and we'll fill in the blanks."

I paused. "What's happening tomorrow? Is Ms. Higgins okay?"

"You'll see it for yourself. And, you'll have an unforgettable night."

"Dress to impress," Sam said.

"Right," Darien agreed. "Look sharp. A tux, if you can."

"A tux?" I took a deep breath and looked at my watch. My half-hour break-time was almost up.

"I don't know about this," I said. "Is Ms. Higgins alright?"

Darien rolled his eyes. "Listen. I know you must be tentative after what you saw, but you weren't supposed to see it. You need to get the whole picture. I can't just have you walk out of here thinking we're criminals. You understand that, don't you?"

There was a tension in the room while I wondered what to say.

"I don't know if I want to be involved."

"You already *are* involved," said Sam sharply. I looked at him. "That's what Darien is trying to tell you. You became involved when you helped us stick Ms. Higgins in the chute."

"What? I didn't help, I didn't even know what the hell you were doing. I still don't. How do I know nobody's going to stick me down a trash chute?"

"Kevin," Darien said, "if we wanted to stick you in a trash chute, don't you think we had the opportunity?"

Sam nodded. In a minute, I nodded too. He was right. They were right.

"Plus," Sam said, "we're putting our asses on the

line here. We're only inviting you because we have to."

"He's right," Darien said. "People pay crazy money to see this. This is big."

"Seriously?" I said.

"No kidding," Darien said. "Be here. Trust me."

God knows, I had nothing to do tomorrow, let alone anything worth crazy money to anyone. The life of a grocery boy. And my life was on the boring end of that spectrum. Plus, it was the only way to put my mind at ease about Ms. Higgins.

"Come on," Darien said. "Tell me you'll be here." He winked at me the way he does.

"Alright," I said. "I'll be here."

Darien nodded. "And Kevin..."

"Yeah?"

"Keep it under your hat. God help you, not a word."

2

I COULDN'T FOCUS on work for the rest of the day, and getting to sleep that night proved impossible. Around midnight I got out of bed and went to look for that tux I knew I had somewhere. I ended up finding it at the bottom of an old bag of clothes in my closet. I found my iron and unwrapped the old cord and set to ironing it out on the rug. Life is strange. Alone at night, in the perfect quiet of my dirty little apartment, there's nothing to distract you from the strangeness.

I've always delivered food. Before starting in the grocery store, I delivered pizza. I was in school at the time, working leisurely towards a liberal arts degree, whatever that is. One sunny day, I arrived at my delivery and got out of the car and just stood there for a minute with the sun on the back of my neck, and the realization just poured right into me. I realized that delivering food was all I really wanted to do. I had no idea what I was doing school-wise, all I knew was I liked my day job. That was almost fifteen years ago, and every dollar I've made since has been from delivering food. Some nights I would sit there, alone and single, wondering what things would have been like if I'd stayed in college. It's funny how your sensibilities change over the years. A pleasant ray of sunshine on the neck of a nineteen-year-old offers no warmth on the cold nights of your mid-thirties. Nineteen is a lousy age for a guy to have a revelation.

By sunrise, I realized I was in no shape to go to work, and I called in sick with my best scratchy voice. After getting a few hours sleep, I made coffee and went outside to grab the paper. Old Mrs.

Henderson was out walking her little designer dog. I can't remember the kind of dog, only that it was absurdly expensive—her husband had left her more money than she could possibly spend anyway. She waved hello, and I stood and waited while she walked over.

"No work today, Kevin?" she said.

"I couldn't sleep last night."

"That's a shame. I hope you feel better."

"I'm alright. Just tired." The little dog was sniffing at my leg. I reached down to pet it.

"How old are you now, Kevin?"

"Thirty-five."

"When are you going to settle down? I'll bet you have all sorts of girlfriends."

"Not a one," I said.

"That surprises me," she said. "They say being married helps you sleep better, you know."

"Hmm. Interesting."

"You might sleep better, that's all."

10:00 pm, Friday, January 16th

As I drove up to the building that night, my heart

thudding in my chest the whole way, a helicopter was descending to the roof, scattering old shards of leaves and debris over the entranceway. I pulled off into the visitor area—this time I had no business in the loading zone. Must be a medical emergency, hope it's not one of my regulars. I got out of the car and watched it come down, my suit jacket billowing in the breeze. It didn't look like a medical helicopter. It was jet black.

I thumbed Darien's extension into the intercom and after a few rings he answered

"Kevin?"

"Yeah, it's me."

"Good, come on in."

It was strange in the building at night. Dead quiet, the exit signs lit bright red, the moonlight in the windows at the end of the wings. I was there nearly every day, but tonight, I felt like an intruder. *What the hell are you doing, Kevin? Turn around and get out of here now. Call the police, you dummy! You witnessed an assault!*

I stopped for a moment in the middle of the hall, listening to the voice of reason in my head. I *had* witnessed an assault. Normally I'd have called the police right away. So why didn't I? Because I was scared? Because I was confused? Or because I was curious? I stood there feeling the hammering of my heart. The blood rushing in my ears. I couldn't remember the last time my heart beat like that. I couldn't remember the last time I felt anything at all. Not since that warm sunbeam landed on the back of my neck and I decided to accept my destiny. I *was* curious. *Irresistibly* curious.

I knocked on the maintenance door and Darien answered right away. Sam was there too, sitting and smoking. They were both looking spiffy in their tuxedos. I had to grin.

"Howdy," Darien said. "Ready for a big night?"

"I don't know what to be ready for."

"You heard the chopper?" asked Sam.

"I saw it land up there, is there an emergency?"

"If I told you who was in it, you'd never believe me."

"Well who is it?"

"You'll see, don't worry." He checked his watch.

"Ms. Higgins alright?"

"She's fine," Darien said.

"Fighting shape," Sam said.

Darien chuckled. "Alright, we ready?"

Sam stood up. "Let's go."

We started towards the door. "But Kevin," Darien said. He held up a finger. "I'm fairly sure it goes without saying, but I have to make it clear. What you saw the other day, what you're going to see tonight, you never tell a soul. Anyone. Ever. Are we in agreement?"

"Yes," I said. At this point, it was implied. A day and-a-half after the incident took place, I was just as guilty as they were for staying quiet as long as I did. But more important than that, I felt something even more powerful than guilt—excitement.

In the elevator, Darien pushed the buttons for floors one and five simultaneously. After holding them a few seconds, the lights dimmed and the elevator began to descend.

"We're going down?" I asked. We'd been on the first floor to begin with. He nodded.

Not only did we go down, but we seemed to go down forever. At some point, I thought I felt us stop, move sideways, and descend again. When we finally did stop, the door opened to a rush of earthy air. We stepped out into some dim concrete tunnel.

"What in the world..."

"Follow me," said Darien, his voice amplified in the throaty corridor. Unseen drips thunked into unseen puddles. As we walked, I sensed rhythmic vibrations resonating through the walls. Ominous at first. Then I realized what it was. Music. Dance music.

At the hall's end was a slab steel door, and Darien stopped me short.

"Almost forgot," he said, and reached into his pocket and pulled out a gold coin the size of a silver dollar. He handed it to me. Embossed on the face was a strange symbol, some kind of intricate sphere.

"If anyone stops you, if anyone asks who you are, just show them the token," he said. "Think of it as your ticket stub."

I put the coin in my pocket.

Sam approached the console, and seven beeps later, a pneumatic hiss, metallic clank, and the door slid open. They both turned to watch my reaction as I looked inside.

Bright spotlights twisted through the dark room, moving in time with the loud music. I stepped forward and looked around. An enormous underground chamber. Full of people. Full of lights. There was clearly a party going on, one of unprecedented size. Darien smiled at me. My eyes must have been the size of dinner plates.

"Come on," Darien said, and they led me down a winding esplanade, dozens and dozens of well-dressed debutantes, laughing and chatting with their drinks. I couldn't tell whether the thumping in my chest was my heart or the pounding bass. We made our way towards what appeared to be the centerpiece of it all, a walled, circular pit, five feet high at the rim, maybe fifty feet deep. At the opening of a wide staircase, you could see down galleries of steep stadium seating funneling around the pit. An amphitheater, all stone and marble. The floor was rimmed with spikes like giant punji sticks, wound and strung with chains. Dimly illuminating the pit were red floodlights, panning the sandy floor. Some unseen crowd of partiers cheered in unison from a writhing galaxy of lights.

"Holy shit," I said.

"Welcome to The Colosseum," Darien said.

I managed to pull my gaze from the pit and looked around at the surrounding pavilions. As my eyes adjusted, the dark revealed scores and scores of sharply-dressed patrons drinking, talking, dancing. Tiki-style bars, blue neon shining brightly in their bar-mirrors. Two topless hula girls swinging around poles made to look like palm trees. A sprawling dance floor encircled the chamber, undulating with dancers. An elevated deejay booth with its little silhouette bouncing back and forth in the flashing lights.

"It's amazing," I said.

Darien and Sam were smiling. Darien leaned close to me so I could hear him. "How about some dinner?"

"I don't get paid for another week," I said.

"Not necessary," Sam said. "It's all included."

The far end of the chamber was much quieter. There were two restaurants, one French, one Japanese, and we all agreed on sushi. A white-faced geisha-waitress took our orders and promptly returned with hot sake and a huge platter of magnificent-looking food."

"You sure this is free?" I said.

"Are you kidding?" Darien said. "You think we could afford this?"

"So what do you think?" Sam said. He tipped back a cup of sake.

"I have no words," I said. I really didn't.

"I'm sure you'll come up with a few," Darien said, pouring a shot into my cup. "Hey, wanna know who that was in the chopper?"

"Sure."

He nodded behind me and I turned to look. It was difficult to see in the dimness, but my eyes adjusted, and there they were.

"Are you kidding me?"

Holding court at a private table on one of the terraced platforms were former presidents Bill Clinton and George Bush. Several tuxedoed men sat with them, and more at nearby tables seemed to be watching in protection.

"They're here every show," Sam said.

"And there," Darien said, pointing at a distant

table.

Squinting, I made out the unmistakable profile of Daniel Stern. He was sitting with John Heard.

"Get out," I said.

"Those two haven't missed a show since C.H.U.D."

"You're sitting in probably the most exclusive place in the country right now," Sam said. "The rich, the famous, and us."

"Not a bad perk, huh?" Darien said. "Guaranteed we're the only janitors in here right now."

"Facilities and maintenance technicians," said Sam. His eyes were starry in the light of the candles—the sake had obviously done its trick.

Darien laughed. "He's one proud janitor."

"I get it," I said. "I'm a delivery engineer."

"Boy, that's a stretch," Sam said.

"I'll give you that," I said. "This is really something, guys. I haven't been out in a long, long time."

"You gotta let loose sometimes," said Darien. "Life is short. Can't spend the whole thing working."

"I'm thinking you're right."

With the alcohol warming my stomach and everything else overwhelming my senses, I hadn't even thought of Ms. Higgins. But that wouldn't last long.

It was midnight when a voice came booming over the PA system.

"Ladies and Gentlemen. Welcome again, to The Colosseum!"

Applause erupted through the circle of the chamber. I followed everyone's gaze to a high buttress overlooking the far side of the room. The way it was designed, it appeared to be floating in midair. On it stood a regally robed figure holding something like a scepter.

"It's the Archon," Darien said.

"In the tradition of The Organization, we select before each event, the next of the twelve. Allow me now to direct your attention to the Sphere of Judgement!"

More applause, and from high above, a huge and dark shape was descending to hang above the pit. As it came into the light, it seemed to blanket the chamber with a reverent hush. Some kind of rust-tortured gyroscope. Through the metallic ribs you could see a shining core, engraved with numbers. I noticed it was the same sphere pictured on the gold token Darien had given me.

With a sound like creaking gears, the core began to move, and gradually picked up to a spin. The Archon then continued.

"As the world spins small and silent under the apathetic stars, mankind waits fearfully in the imminence of death. But we, The Organization, understand there can be no light without darkness, no life without death. So with death, we celebrate life!"

"For The Organization!" chanted the crowd.

"What's this about?" I asked Darien.

He leaned in close. "Twelve new combatants over the course of a year. Before every show, the Sphere of Judgement picks the next selectee."

"Wait, so Ms. Higgins was—"

"Last month's selectee to be tonight's combatant."

Combatant? What is she going to do, play bingo?

The core of the Sphere of Judgement was spinning fast, the numbers flying by too quick to read. The Archon raised his scepter and brought it down with a sound like a judge's gavel. The core began to wind down, and eventually, the numbers became legible.

"So each month," Darien said, "it's a one in five-hundred chance to get selected."

I was watching the numbers flick by as the core lost its momentum. It was almost hypnotic to. The Archon continued.

"Tonight, midnight of the third Friday of the first month of the year, we have for you: Agatha M. Higgins, number 209, seventy-eight years of age, and our champion, Helen R. Shoemaker, number 445, seventy-four years of age. As always, the prize of victory is..."

"To live to fight another day!" chanted the crowd.

I saw Daniel Stern and John Heard high-five over at their table.

The numbers were moving slower now. Slower. Slower. Then they stopped. In the rusty window showed number 284.

"Apartment 284?" I said. "That's Charlie." I didn't know if I was supposed to be happy for him or what. He never had any luck at bingo, I knew that much.

"Charlie's it," Darien said. "Next month, he fights

tonight's winner."

"What do you mean, fight?"

"Fight," said Sam. "What else would it mean?"

"Well, what does it mean? A debate? A cook-off?"

"Number 284," said the Archon. "Charles Vandergrift. Seventy-nine years of age."

The audience applauded. President Clinton had that pleased smile of his, clapping and nodding approvingly. President Bush patted him on the thigh and whispered something in his ear.

I recalled Ms. Higgins then, the way Sam and Darien had carried her out of her apartment. I couldn't picture Charlie like that. Were they planning to stuff him down the trash chute too?

"Are you guys going to do that...thing to Charlie?"

They looked at each other. "Not if we don't have to," Sam said.

"Ms. Higgins is a feisty one," Darien said. "She never leaves her apartment, didn't want to yesterday either. The feisty ones take the chute. The agreeable ones, we can usually get them into the elevator quietly enough."

After the three of us finished dinner, we went to

our seats; simple stools next to the stadium's maintenance entrance with a clear view of the pit. I supposed we were going to see some kind of competition. Maybe some kind of performance art. Either that, or there was some metaphor here I just wasn't getting.

People filed from the bars down the stairs into the amphitheater. Everyone leased their own seats, Darien had told me. They cost more the closer you got to the bottom, but even the nosebleeds were obscenely expensive. Bush's and Clinton's, which were near ground-level, were two-hundred thousand apiece. To get in at all, you needed to know somebody. Then you had to crank open your wallet. Darien reiterated how he and Sam had the best deal in the house, and reminded me how lucky I was to be there with them.

The crowd grew steadily quieter and the air grew stiff with tension. Just as I checked my watch to see it was 12:30 am, red floodlights filled the pit. Smoke machines poured a creeping mist out onto the sand. Up on his flying buttress of sorts, the Archon sat on a throne. He lifted his scepter and brought it down with a loud crack.

"Ladies and gentlemen, the time has come! Allow me to introduce your competitors for the evening. First, our challenger!"

Darien elbowed me and gestured to a gate on the left side of the pit. The gate's vertical bars were sinking into the floor. When they'd disappeared entirely, sand rushing in to seal the holes, out she hobbled. I recognized her immediately for her darkly dyed bouffant, now opaque and purple in the bright floodlights. She wore the same floral dress she'd had on when Darien and Sam pushed her down the trash chute. Old Ms. Higgins looked in fine spirits. Only one peculiarity. Her arms were fitted to the elbows with what appeared to be enormous chainsaws.

"Get the hell outta here," I said. My heart rate doubled in an instant. The audience was applauding and whistling and leaping out of their seats. Chants began: *Chainsaw...Chainsaw...Chainsaw...* Even Darien and Sam were up and chanting.

And just when I thought things couldn't get any crazier, Ms. Higgins thrust her chainsaw-arms up in the air and they went off like jet engines, little

111

streams of oily smoke joining the mist of the fog machines. The chants gave way to lunatic applause. I stared at Ms. Higgins's face, but saw no apprehension, no fear, not even a hint of distraction from all the ruckus. Nice old Ms. Higgins, who always ordered pop tarts when her grandkids were coming to visit. And what I saw in her eyes now was something like...determination?

"How is she lifting those things?" I asked Darien. "She can't even put away her pop tarts."

"Weighing in at one-hundred-fifty-seven pounds, seventy-eight years old, one-time widow. She enjoys cooking and knitting afghans, but tonight, she's trying her hand—both hands, in fact—at butchery! Fighting to the death, Ms. Agatha Higgins!"

The stadium blew over with a hollow rumble. I was still trying to grasp what I was seeing. She didn't even seem to be holding onto the chainsaws, her arms were just kind of *made* into them. The skin was badly bruised where they wedged into the gauntlets that held them on. Don't they know she's on blood thinners?

"And introducing our champion. Seventy-four

years young, and one hot cookie. Widow of three, murderer of two, but this hot mama don't make shoes! She collects oven mitts and enjoys ballroom dancing. And boy oh boy, this gal really cooks on the dance floor! Defending her title as two-time Bloodbath Colosseum Champion, "Helen "Barbecue" Shoemaker!"

The crowd erupted once again. A gate lowered opposite Ms. Higgins, and out she stepped, Mrs. Shoemaker, a pilot light glowing at the end of each armored arm. Hoses ran to a tank mounted on her back. She lifted her arms and let loose two gouts of fire. The stench of gas rolled over the stands on rippling waves of heat.

"Jesus," I said. "I thought she'd died."

"I'm taking the champ," Darien said.

"She's a three-to-one favorite," Sam said. "But you never know. Shoemaker's got the range, but if Higgins gets in there, all it takes is one good swing. Those saws are a sonofabitch."

"So without further delay...For The Organization!"

The crowd chanted: "For The Organization!"

I looked around; the crowd in their fancy dress and

unbridled excitement. The smoke rising off the floor of the pit below. The electric charge in the air of the arena. My mouth felt dry, and I realized it was hanging open. *They aren't really going to—*

"Fight!" The Archon swung his scepter and a gong sounded throughout the chamber. Suddenly, Ms. Higgins charged, one chainsaw leveled, one cocked back behind her head. I'd never seen her move beyond a geriatric shuffle, and now she bounded through the sand like a cheetah. Then she swung. Hard. A whirring haymaker. Mrs. Shoemaker barely ducked in time. She rolled over in the sand, tank and all.

I happened to know Mrs. Shoemaker's hips were ravaged by osteoporosis and arthritis. One day she'd ordered double-sided tape with her groceries, and when I showed up, she talked me into securing the safety-seat to the floor around her toilet. For a half-hour, I heard all about her numerous health issues while I taped the aluminum rack to the tiles. I was sad when I heard she'd died, but hardly surprised. *Now,* I was surprised.

Impossibly, she sprung up behind Mrs. Higgins, on

what must have been a brand-new pair of legs. Ms. Higgins was still recovering from the momentum of her big swing, and Mrs. Shoemaker clobbered her over the right ear with her big, bionic arm. Ms. Higgins spun twice and went down. Shoemaker aimed both flamethrowers and bathed the sand in fire. The crowd winced at the sudden burst of bright flame, but when they receded, Higgins had gotten out of the way. She was back up and poised to swing.

Shoemaker ducked, barely dodging another haymaker. She stumbled away, trying to open up enough space to counter-attack, but Higgins was all over her. Shoemaker swung wildly, the flamethrower trailing a loop of blue flame. Higgins avoided getting clubbed, but winced with a faceful of fire. She'd been burned. The crowd roared.

"Ooh, clipped her," said Darien.

But Ms. Higgins didn't seem to mind being scorched, and continued her charge, aiming a buzzing saw at Mrs. Shoemaker's midsection. Shoemaker parried, but a loud, metallic clank sent them both rebounding and there was a split second of confusion as they regained their bearings. I realized I was digging my fingernails into my thighs.

The crowd gasped. The blunder had opened up a fair amount of space and Mrs. Shoemaker aimed both arms at her target. Darien elbowed me excitedly. It looked like this was it. For the first time, Mrs. Higgins raised her saws in defense.

"Here it is, here it is," said Darien.

Shoemaker fired. Dwindling squirts of burning gas dribbled onto the sand. The crowd gasped again. Quickly, everyone understood what had happened. The tank. Ms. Higgins had clipped the tank. The pressure was gone. Mrs. Shoemaker was dumbstruck.

Ms. Higgins wasted no time. She closed the distance and struck. Shoemaker raised an arm, which was promptly bisected at the elbow. It seemed to wait a moment before bleeding, then sprayed blood in gouts. The audience was out of their seats.

Ms. Higgins continued her assault, severing the other arm at the shoulder, then her left leg mid-shin, tipping her into the sand. More shocking still was Mrs. Shoemaker's face. She was disappointed. Not horrified, not even resigned—she looked like she'd just burned the roast with the dinner guests waiting at the table. Ms. Higgins, conversely, glowed like she'd just solved the puzzle on *Wheel of Fortune*.

The lights shined brightly on Mrs. Shoemaker's paling skin. Flowing blood gleamed bright, then soaked dully into the sand. Ms. "Help me, young man" Agatha Higgins, wearing a goodnatured grin on her charred face, was carving up Mrs. Shoemaker like a turkey. Finally, she raised an arm high, then brought it down through her opponent and into the sand, where the saw ground to a halt. There was so little blood left in Mrs. Shoemaker, her head rolled off with barely a drip.

I don't normally drink much, but tonight, I needed it. After watching the Archon crown Mrs. Higgins the new champion and teasing her upcoming match against Charlie Vandergrift, everyone made their way back to the terraces and pavilions. The deejays turned on the music, and the dancers resumed dancing. Bartenders poured drinks, waitresses weaved between tables. At the center of it all, the contents of Mrs. Shoemaker left a brown splotch on the arena floor.

I was quiet as we returned to our table. It wasn't only that I didn't know what to say. It was that I seemed to be the only one horrified by all of this. I was scared that I'd be found out. They'd realize I didn't belong here. Then what would happen?

Daniel Stern was gesticulating crazily over at the bar. John Heard was clearly amused.

"So what'd you think?" Darien said. "Man, I'm jazzed right now."

"Great fight," said Sam.

No words came to me. I had to say something about it, I just didn't know what.

Darien examined my face and tipped back a shot of Jaegermeister. "It's fucked, right?"

I looked at him.

"You can say what you're thinking, you don't have to hide it." He gestured around the arena. "Everyone here is aware that the ethics are questionable."

"Questionable?"

"Listen. I know how it looks, we all saw this for the first time too once. But there's more to this than you think."

George Bush was unfolding a wad of bills and counting them out to Bill Clinton. I guess he'd bet on Mrs. Shoemaker.

"There's no public funding, Kev. Donations don't pay for this building. The Organization does."

The waitress came by, and we ordered another round of drinks. I asked for a double, then changed it to a triple. "How long has this has been going on, Darien?"

"At this building here? Since the beginning. But The Organization itself?" He tapped his fingers on the table and looked at Sam.

"Since Caesar," Sam said.

3

I'VE BEEN AT THE GROCERY STORE for nine
years now. Delivering the home-shopping stuff is
where I'm the most comfortable. I like it out on the
road. Behind the shelves of the store is all the
darkness of the food business.

We have our own in-house butcher, and I've
watched him cut pigs into all their more commonly-
known parts. By the time the pigs arrive, they've
been mercifully removed of all character. Headless,
footless, tail-less, bloodless. Bleached, empty bodies.

Without an imagination, you can hack them apart with comfortable apathy. Lenny, the butcher, has no imagination. "It's all product to me," he says.

My imagination has never been much help to me. I can't even make peace with fruits and vegetables. There's something offensive about the mileage of a salad. Lettuce from Mexico, cabbage from Guatemala, celery from Uzbekistan. Eating a salad feels to me like an unreasonable demand for attention.

Processed meat is worse still. I have no problem eating the less-favorable parts of an animal. It has a kind of Native-American gratitude to it, letting no part of the animal go to waste. The perversion of a hot dog, however, is in the collective deaths to create it. One bite could fathomably contain the flesh of a thousand creatures. We seem to know a hot dog is ugly, at least subconsciously we do. We hide it in a bun and pile it over with condiments and eat it without looking. We're watching sports.

It isn't just the food that doesn't sit right with me, it's the whole waxy, yellowed environment of the grocery store. Even the instrumental renditions piping from the ceiling sound waxy and yellowed. When I was a kid, I remember wondering what an anti-gravity walk up there might be like. To me, it looks like a bomb-blown city landscape painted white.

And no one but the shoppers are happy to be here; least happy of all may be the soda merchandisers. They cart up loads and loads of soda and drag it into the soda aisle to fill the shelves. I notice a lot of them have their wrists wrapped. They leave to stock another store for a few hours, then come back to the first, where the shelves have already been emptied, and stock them all over again. There's a built-in futility to it that eliminates all gratification beyond pay. The fourth level of Dante's hell, where the greedy push their boulders up the hills only to have them roll back down. This is the life of the soda merchandiser.

I once saw a Coke guy pushing one cart in front of him while pulling another behind; a technique they call "walk like an Egyptian". The Egyptians knew how to move some heavy stuff, but the pictures are a poor demonstration of actual ergonomics. You could hear the disk snap in his spine before he spilled out on the linoleum. Since then, I've been extra careful with my back.

Recently, I asked a Pepsi merchandiser what the hardest part of the job was. I imagined he would bring up the hot trailers, the heavy bottles, maybe even the unrelenting elevator music. But he'd had more time to consider my question than I thought.

"The pointlessness of life," he said.

I can relate to that. The life of a working schlub can be boring. But after seeing the trouble a little excitement can get you into, the whole point seems a little different.

Three weeks had gone by since the Organization thing; one more week until the next ceremony. I'd run into Darien five or six times, who kept asking me if I was coming again.

"Don't underestimate Mrs. Higgins," he told me. "Sure, Charlie's got her in the size department, but listen... She's down there right now getting the champion's treatment. Might be new weapons, might be who-knows-what. Charlie's up here scratching his balls, no idea what's going on."

I told him I'd be there. I tried to feign enthusiasm. I was afraid that if I didn't, he'd begin to distrust me. Who knows what he'd do if he thought I was a rat. I'd already seen him tie up an old lady and stuff her down a garbage hole. He wasn't averse to seeing people die either, so what would stop him from killing me?

Come Friday, I'd tell him I was sick. Maybe I'd even tell him to bet a couple bucks on Charlie for me, just to throw him off. The coward I am. And Charlie. Poor Charlie...

I saw Charlie in the common room at least several times a week. I couldn't help being morose when we chatted, and it wasn't lost on him.

"You sure you're alright, son? Look a little pale. When was the last time you took yourself a vacation?"

"You should take vitamins," said Beattie, apartment 127. "Do you take vitamins?"

"I'm alright," I told them both.

"I told the doctor I've been putting steak in the blender. So he tells me, Charlie, you ever try

Salisbury steak? I said no, so he tells me to give it a try. And you know what, it isn't so bad. And it goes down pretty easy."

"Helen said not to eat those Salisbury steaks. They're full of salt."

"So's the ocean. And the fish are fine, aren't they?"

"I never thought of that," Beattie said.

I can't explain why, but Charlie's comment about the Salisbury steaks struck a nerve in me. Maybe because it was some rare good news. He found something he liked, something he enjoyed. Even if that was all the good news he'd ever have—even if a salty, Hungryman TV dinner was the only thing he lived for, it still meant he had *something* to live for.

But that wasn't all he lived for. He did things. He liked coming down to the common room, chatting with the other residents, listening to the record player. He liked saying hi to me when I showed up with a delivery. And I was just going to let this happen to him? I couldn't.

"Charlie, listen. We have to talk. Somewhere private."

Charlie had never heard my tone of voice this way.

"What is it, son?"

"Can we just go somewhere else a minute?"

"Well, sure, I suppose, lemme just get up."

I helped him up and we walked down the hall to the laundry room. Luckily, no one was in there.

"Are you alright, son?"

"Yeah, I'm fine, it's nothing like that, it's...I have to get you out of here."

"What? How do you mean?"

I checked around to make doubly sure no one was around. He watched me concernedly.

"Charlie, you're not safe here. You have to leave."

"What? Son, I don't get it."

"I can't explain it to you right now, at least not here. You've just got to trust me. Just trust me."

Charlie's face was somewhere between confused and concerned. "You know me," I said. "I'll explain it to you later. Just grab what you need, and I'll get you whatever else you need. But I have to get you out of here. Today."

I admit, it took some effort to maintain my resolve for the rest of the day. I'd start to lose my nerve, then remind myself how I felt back in the common room.

I have to do what little I can. I can't go up against the Archon. I can't go up against Bush, and Clinton, and the cast of C.H.U.D., and who knows who else. I can't even defend myself against Darien and Sam if it comes down to it—I'll end up at the bottom of a trash bin. I just want to save Charlie. *One thing at a time. Save Charlie.*

Charlie packed a bag of essentials and met me out by the loading area at 6:00 pm, where I sat with my lights off. I helped him into my car and we left around the back of the building.

"Did anyone see you leave?" I said.

"Everybody's in the game room that woulda seen me. It's card night."

"Good."

My heart was pounding. *Relax,* I told myself. *You made it.*

"So you gonna tell me what the problem is or what?" Charlie had shaved and put on aftershave. I felt guilty for rushing him out of his home, even though I knew I was saving his life. A guy Charlie's age shouldn't have to be dragged around like this.

"You're not going to believe me. I can barely believe

127

it. I saw it and I *still* can't believe it."

"Well come out with it son. I can barely believe I just let the delivery man kidnap me."

I glanced over at him. "Remember Helen? Shoemaker?"

"Sure. Poor gal passed away a few months back. We had coffee a time or two."

"She didn't die three months ago. She died one month ago."

Charlie paused a moment. "How do you mean? They had the funeral—"

"She was killed. Last month."

Charlie was silent for a minute. I felt his gaze on me as I drove. I wished he'd just stop right there with the questions. I wished he'd just trust me.

"Son? How do you know that?"

"Remember Nettie? Apartment 424? They killed her too."

"Who do you mean *they?* Who killed them?"

"The Organization, they call themselves. They force people to kill each other under the building. They kill twelve people a year. And you were next."

"That's crazy talk!"

"I know how it sounds, Charlie. But it's true. I saw Mrs. Shoemaker die."

Charlie was quiet again.

"Say it's true, what you're saying. What happened?"

So I told him. I told him the whole story, and finished just as we pulled around back of my place and parked the car. I turned off the car and looked at him, waiting for his reaction.

"Son, I'm not good at many things, but I can smell bullshit for miles. Always could, still can."

"You don't believe me?"

"I'm not saying that. Because I at least know you believe it. And I'd be lying if I said you didn't scare me. Because you did. For one reason or another."

"I'm not letting it happen. Not to you."

"Thank you, son. But what now?"

"I don't know. We'll figure it out."

The old man sitting in my living room chair wasn't the same Charlie I knew from the retirement home. He didn't say much, he mostly just sat and watched the TV. I made him a frozen Salisbury steak dinner, and sat with him while he ate. It took him a long time to eat it. How did they expect this old man to get into that pit and fight for his life?

Then again, Ms. Higgins could barely lift a grocery bag, and she wielded those chainsaws like some kind of murderous lumberjack. How was it possible? It was all just so bizarre.

"Kevin?" Charlie was wiping his mouth with a napkin.

"Yeah?"

"What am I supposed to do?"

"I don't know. We'll figure something out."

"You really sure about all this gobbledygook you were telling me?"

"If I wasn't, I never would've dragged you out of your home like that."

"So when can I go back?"

"You don't want to go back, Charlie, I saw what they wanted to do to you."

"Because I have nowhere else to go."

"I know it, I know. I just have to figure it out, that's all."

He paused for a moment. "But what if you're wrong about all this?"

"I know what I saw."

We didn't speak for awhile. I looked online for other fully-subsidized homes for the elderly, but there were none anywhere. Even if there had been, I remembered what Darien told me—there aren't enough donations to keep a place like that running. And if I did find another free rest home, what if it had its own Organization? Maybe the same Organization.

Inevitably, the grim truth became clear. Charlie truly had nowhere else to go.

When I came home from work Wednesday, Charlie was sitting in front of the TV. My apartment had begun to smell like his favorite aftershave lotion. Two days until the next Organization ceremony. In forty-eight hours, Charlie was scheduled to fight to the death. And here he was, watching Jeopardy in my apartment.

"Heya Charlie," I said. "I got you more TV dinners."

He turned to me with sallow eyes, shiny in the light of the TV set. "Son, I know you mean well and all. But I've had some of time to think, and...well, I think I'm gonna go ahead and go back home."

I wasn't surprised to hear him say it. None of us had come up with any plans. I'd had several deliveries to the building in the past few days, and people had noticed he was gone, including Sam and Darien.

Darien was vacuuming the hall when I ran into him the day before. He seemed distraught, and I knew why.

"Guess who's missing?" he said.

"Who?"

He checked to be sure no one was around. "This month's combatant."

"Charlie? Where'd he go?" I wanted to swallow, but willed my throat still.

"I was hoping you'd know," he said. "If I don't have him by Thursday, I don't know what's going to happen. You sure you have no idea at all? Sam's losing his mind over it."

"Haven't seen or heard from him."

Darien sighed and shook his head. "Christ, they're gonna kill me if I don't deliver him on time."

"They'll kill you?"

"Look. I've got this general rule I like to follow. And

that rule is: don't piss off Archon Bloodbath.

"Can't they just pick someone else?"

"Stats are up, bets are placed...and this has never happened before. The Archon's not going to like it." He looked in my eyes. "You sure you have no idea? You know him pretty well, don't you?"

"I wouldn't say that, I chat with him here and there."

"Let me know if you hear anything, okay? It takes twenty-four hours to get done whatever they do to these old folks. If I don't produce Charlie by Thursday, I don't know what they're going to do about it. And I don't know what's going to happen to me and Sam either."

It was hard not to feel sorry for Darien at the time, evil as the whole thing was. But now, it looked like he might get his man after all. If Charlie believed a word of what I'd told him, he'd never want to go back. He must think I've lost my mind. But I can't just let him do this to himself, it's suicide. If I let him go back, it's practically homicide by negligence.

"Charlie, listen. If you go back, they're going to get you. Plus, you have to understand the situation you're putting *me* in right now."

"I know what you think, son."

"Do you think I'm crazy?"

"I think you're a fine man. But I don't have the energy for this. Not to mention I don't have a whole lot of time left anyhow. And I appreciate everything, I just...I gotta get on."

"I can't force you to stay, but you're asking me to—"

"Son, I'll be fine. I just called the maintenance boys, one of them's set to pick me up in an hour."

My stomach went sour. I don't know what my face looked like just then, but Charlie sure picked up on it.

"Hey, don't worry," Charlie said. "I didn't tell them about any of the gobbledygook you told me. I only told them you offered to put me up awhile."

"Charlie, no more messing around, we have to get the hell out of here. Right now."

"What do you mean? I told you I'm going home."

"Is that your final choice? Because we don't have time right now to argue about this."

"I'm sorry son. I've been thinking a lot about it, and well...I really think you need that vacation."

It was no use. I told Charlie to lock the door on his way out, and that I was going to stay with my brother in Bethesda. I have no brother in Bethesda, no surviving family at all, so when they dragged that information out of Charlie, maybe they'd go looking for me in the wrong places.

It started raining just as I left. Running down the back alley behind the house, leaving my apartment and my car and all my belongings behind, it struck me the same way it had when I'd gotten out of the car with that fateful pizza delivery the day I decided on my destiny. I had no control over my destiny. I had no control over what happened to me. I had no control over what happened to other people. I had no control over anything at all.

Ducking from headlights, I found my way through backyards, alleys and dimly-lit arteries to the old motor lodge by the highway. The yard was full of tractor trailers, and I weaved my way through the dark to the office. It was 9:00 pm, and I knew they had Charlie by now. I assumed they already knew I'd told him everything, and by now, he knew I'd told him the truth after all. He must be scared to death.

The room was small and dusty and smelled like stale cigarette smoke, but at least it was dry. I sat on the edge of the bed, just thinking. What was next? Where would I go? Did I have to change my name? How the hell did I get into this giant mess?

I never asked for any of this. I never meant to happen upon a kidnapping, I never asked to be invited to some geriatric death match. All I wanted to do was deliver groceries, and when the situation called for it, to save one old man. Was that too much to ask? Had I completely derailed the wheel of fortune? Or was this my destiny after all?

When the adrenaline finally subsided, I was so drained, so exhausted, I lay down and passed out in my wet clothes. I don't remember falling sleep.

4

NIGHTS ARE CRUEL sometimes. When I started delivering pizza, I had this recurring nightmare where I'd have a ton of deliveries in my car and get completely lost for hours and hours. It happened from time to time where you'd be a little late, and even that stressed me out immensely, but nothing like these nightmares of mine. In the dreams, I'd be passing signs that said: "Last Exit Before Tennessee," and "Welcome To Pennsylvania." It was always a relief to wake up from dreams like that.

I had no dreams that night, but waking up was no relief either. I woke to cold and damp. I reached to pull up the covers but my arm refused to move. Must have slept on it wrong. But no, I tried turning over and found I couldn't move at all. I was completely immobilized. Tied down.

I panicked, struggled with all my strength. I fought against the leathery bindings, twisting my wrists, wringing the flesh of my arms, but it was no use. Eventually I gave up and just lay there with my chest heaving. I wanted to believe it was a dream, but the earthy, dank smell proved to me what I didn't want to believe. I remembered it from the moment those elevator doors opened up. They'd found me. I was underground.

It wasn't long before I heard approaching footsteps. The echoing click of hard shoes on concrete. I willed myself still, hoping they'd pass and there would be quiet again. But they stopped at their loudest and a lock clicked and a door swung open and three figures stood silhouetted by the light behind. Two enormous figures and a smaller one in between.

"Mister Kevin," a man said, and a dim bulb illuminated overhead.

The two large men stepped forward and stood cross-armed on either side of me. They wore leather and mail, some kind of bizarre armor. Then the smaller man stepped into the light, a sharply-featured man in an expensive suit. He glared at me with eyes like scalpels. At a glance, I knew he was evil. And I knew I was helpless to hide my fear.

"Mister Kevin. First of all, I'd like to thank you for exposing a weakness in the security of our operation. If it weren't for Mister Vandergrift's phone call, I believe we'd have had to select a different combatant for tomorrow's ceremony. This would have been an insult to The Organization's traditions. All selectees *must* do battle on their designated date."

He paused. I don't know if he expected me to answer him, but I was unable to.

"I understand you have some affinity for Mister Vandergrift? Some reason you'd rather not see him do battle in the arena tomorrow evening?"

"I know Charlie," I said.

"I see. And is your fondness for Mister Vandergrift

so great that you would be willing to take his place?"

We met eyes. I shivered. His gaze was reptilian. No humanity in those eyes to appeal to, only some brutal operating system, waiting for my answer.

"No," I said.

"I didn't think so."

"Are you the Archon?" I asked.

"Apt, young Kevin. So it's all up to me what to do with you."

"I promise I'll never tell anyone..."

"Your friend Darien assured me you said that a month ago. Long before you told Mister Vandergrift."

"I made a mistake..."

He came closer. "I understand you were in attendance at the last ceremony. Did you see all those people? Hundreds, and only *one* has managed to make such a mistake. A bad, bad mistake."

He stared me down with those eyes again.

"Luckily for you, Mister Kevin, I have a code I operate by. I'm not a sentimental man. Or an empathetic man. Just a man with a code. And because you brought attention to a weak link in the security of my Organization, my code demands I grant you some measure of leniency. Ordinarily, I'd use you for more haphazard experimentation. But for your exciting little fire drill, and the unusual fact that you are alone—we know you have no brother in Bethesda, sans friends, sans family, a solitary man— you'll be recommended for a unique position."

"Listen about this whole Charlie thing—"

"Sentinels, stand him up."

With the sound of a motor, the platform I was secured to began to stand up. As I came face-to-face with the three men, I saw the true size of the masked sentinels. They must have been over seven feet tall. The Archon, who appeared to be a shorter man at first, was at least as tall as me.

"Since the dawn of biomechatronics, the elderly have proved our most convenient pool of subjects, specifically those who should not be missed. But with all the progress in the field, our most notable client is eager for younger, more durable specimens."

"Durable? Me?"

"You should thank the Gods I have some use for you. As for your careless friends, Mister Darien and

Mister Samuel, I had no use for them anymore."

"Please don't hurt me," I said.

"Hurt?" said Archon Bloodbath. "It won't hurt, Mister Kevin. Not yet..."

They wheeled me out into the hall, upright, but still strapped down.

"Oh, Mister Kevin..."

I turned to look back at the Archon. He was holding out a gold coin.

"I hope you don't mind, but I thought I'd take this back. As an employee, you'll no longer be needing it."

"Where are you taking me?" I asked the sentinels, but they paid me no attention. We reached an elevator, got in, and to my shock, descended even deeper into the earth.

We emerged into what looked like a laboratory setting. None of the wet-dirt redolence of the upper levels, but bright, clean, and antiseptic. They rolled me through florescent hallways lined with labs, maybe medical labs. Was this where they treated battle-injured combatants? I stayed quiet.

We came to a stop outside a set of double doors

and went inside. Shortly, I had a lot of attention on me. People in masks and lab coats—doctors, I supposed—came over to examine me. The sentinels left without a word.

"Where am I?" I asked as they unstrapped me, but they wouldn't acknowledge me either. They looked in my eyes with their scopes, in my ears, in my mouth. One felt my throat with his scaly hands. Another roughly performed a hernia test. In fact, "cough" was the only word said to me. After jotting some notes on a clipboard, the doctors vanished, and I was left sitting on a cot, alone with my thoughts. After awhile, I tried not to think at all.

Some time later the door opened, and in stepped a man dressed in military attire carrying a briefcase. He said nothing at first, only watched me with hard blue eyes while he paced the room. It was like he wanted to see me from all angles. Eventually, his face softened and he spoke. "I'm General Boesch of the USBDP."

"I'm Kevin."

"Are you satisfied with your life?"

"I'm...I'm sorry?"

He stopped. "I'm sorry what?"

It took me a moment to understand what he was getting at.

"Sir. I'm sorry sir."

"Are you satisfied with your life?"

"No. No sir, not particularly."

He began pacing again, left, then right. "When you look back at the way you spent your formative years, are you happy with your contribution to humanity? Are you proud of yourself?"

"No sir."

He nodded. "Not many people are. Most of them you have to ask a few times, but they'll usually admit they aren't. They tell me they're proud of themselves the first time I ask, but when I ask them again, they admit it. It's because those dirtbags never bothered to consider it in the first place. You go to school?"

"I dropped out, sir. To deliver pizza. Now I deliver groceries."

"So I've heard. You've been a regular profligate, but at least you know it." He seemed to size me up as he walked back and forth; to decide if I was worth anything. His eyes were as intense as the mirror-shine of his boots.

"You got a good back, kid?"

"Never had any problems, sir."

"I'll bet we can get that puny body under a thousand pounds of steel with the right panactivatory activation implant."

"Implant?"

"We'll let Merle have his fun with you first of course—we owe the old poop some kind of finder's fee."

"I'm confused, sir."

"I believe you met Merle. But do yourself a favor and just call him Archon. Last combatant that called him Merle, well, let's just say he never made it to the arena." He set down his briefcase and snapped open the latches and removed a folder and tossed it on the cot next to me. *Property of the USBDP*, it said.

"Have a look," he said, and threw me a pen. I caught it.

He nodded. "That's for signing the papers. Just a formality, kid, not like you've got much choice in the matter. Just be a good soldier and accept your destiny." He motioned that I open the folder, so I opened it and looked inside. There was no sense asking any more questions. The picture was vague, but the shape was clear.

"Anyway, when you're done playing with Merle, we'll see if you can't make good with that life you wasted. Maybe do some good for your country."

He walked out of the room. I stared at the cover sheet:

United States Biomechatronic Deathtrooper Program

5

I'M NOT SURE IF IT'S TRUE, but I've heard they now breed chickens without beaks. I suppose without a beak to peck with, they'd offer less resistance on the way to the nugget-maker. I've heard they breed them without feathers too, although others have told me the feathers are filler for the nuggets. Feathers in the nuggets don't bother me—again, it has an American-Indian practicality to it. Disturbing is the idea that they can pluck the feathers right out of the DNA.

Incidentally, Americans eat eight billion chickens a year. That's a lot of chickens. I tried to figure out how many nuggets that is, but if I were any good at math, I'd probably be doing something else for a living. And if I was doing something else for a living, I probably wouldn't be thinking about chickens, and other unsavory bits of the food industry. I also never would have ended up in this situation. But there's no sense thinking that way—like General Boesch said, be a good soldier and accept your destiny.

"As the world spins small and silent under the apathetic stars, mankind waits fearfully in the imminence of death. But we, The Organization understand there can be no light without darkness, no life without death. So with death, we celebrate life!"

"For The Organization!"

"Tonight, midnight of the third Friday of the second month of the year, we have for you, our champion, Agatha M. Higgins, number 209, seventy-eight years of age, and our challenger, Charles Vandergrift, number 284, seventy-nine years of age. But hold your bets! Tonight, we have an extra-special treat. I know we rarely stray from our traditions here, but times change, and so must The Organization. So tonight, we meet a new breed of entertainer. From the always-working, always-improving labs of the USBDP, a new prototype tonight is put to the test. Allow me to introduce, at thirty-five years young, this grocery guru is specially equipped to deliver the goods. Previously weighing in at one hundred sixty-five pounds, now a svelte four hundred fifty pounds in his Class Eleven DTB, please welcome to Bloodbath Colosseum...Mister Kevin!"

The gate poles sunk into the sand. This was my cue. I stomped out into the bone-strewn desert of the arena floor, my armored legs moving both heavily and nimbly. All I had to do was walk; somehow, hundreds of pounds of steel followed suit. The crowd went wild, each of which consumed an average of twenty-seven chickens per year.

The armor covered everything but my head and midsection. My arms were clad to the shoulders in similar steel armor, each finger of each oven-door-sized glove tipped with a shining blade the length of a machete, all dragging in the sand behind me. I felt distinctly that the hardware was fastened directly into my bone structure. I suppose it hurt, but it was no bother. Pain was not what it used to be. I could feel it, but it was nothing more than a diagnostic tool to assess my condition.

No fear. Whatever pulsed through my brain and body now prohibited this emotion. Also prohibited were the importances of right and wrong. I knew the difference, it's just that neither one seemed more important than the other. All that mattered was my job. My new job—to annihilate the competition. The trick of the implant was not lost on me. I was fully conscious of what it was doing to me. *Amazing,* what it was doing to me.

"And welcome the challenger and champion, seventy-eight and seventy-nine, respectively, traditionally outfitted in Class Ten Deathtrooper Biomechatronics, Agatha Higgins and Charles Vandergrift!"

The opposite gates went down, and out they came. Ms. Higgins and Charlie both had the same twin-chainsaw getup that Agatha used a month ago. My vision was so sharp, I could count the teeth on the blades. I could count the wrinkles on their faces. I could count them all at once. My hearing was so acute, I could make out individual voices in the din of the crowd. "This is gonna be a slobberknocker, John!" said Daniel Stern. "You betcha, Dan," said John Heard.

"Son?"

I met eyes with Charlie across the pit. He wore the same unconcerned look I knew I had on my face. The loudspeaker boomed with the voice of the Archon:

"For the first time in the history of The Organization, it's a two-on-one match up!" As always, the prize of victory is..."

"To live to fight another day!" chanted the crowd. "For The Organization!"

"Son?"

"Yeah, Charlie?"

"You were right."

I chuckled. "Kinda goes without saying at this point, doesn't it?"

"Right about what?" said Ms. Higgins.

"He told me about this whole thing. I thought he was crackers."

"He's a nice young man. He's not crackers."

"That's what I'm trying to tell him, Agatha."

"I understand, Charlie" I said. "It must've sounded crazy at the time. It is crazy."

"And you know what I was thinking earlier— Colosseum Retirement Home? How didn't I notice anything strange about that?"

"About what?" said Ms. Higgins.

"The name," Charlie said. He gestured around with a chainsaw. "Look. It's a colosseum. Get it?"

"Oh my," she said.

"I just thought it was a name," Charlie said, "like the Rosenfeld Law Firm, over by the A&P."

"You know Harriet?" Ms. Higgins said. "From the fourth floor there? She used to do filing for Mister Rosenfeld."

"Is that right? Anyway son, sorry for not believing you."

"He's your son?"

"No Agatha, he's the delivery man."

"I never had children."

"That's alright, Charlie. I understand."

"And thanks for the Salisbury steaks. You know, the thing about those Salisbury steaks is they're kinda soft. Like someone chewed 'em already for you."

"You're welcome."

"Do you have a girlfriend?" Ms. Higgins said. "I'll bet you have all sorts of girlfriends."

"Not a one."

"That's a shame. You should have a nice girlfriend. You're not...you know?"

"He's not a *mary,* Agatha... You're not, are you?"

"No, no. I guess I just never really met anyone."

"The food here is wonderful, Charlie. Have you tried the pot roast?"

"They gave me a turkey dinner, but they had to put the turkey in the food processor machine. And I'm still waiting for my pills, they never got 'em from my room."

"The pot roast is fabulous, it just falls right apart."

The crowd was in a steady uproar. I zeroed in on George Bush and Bill Clinton. George was showing Bill his new earring. He'd just got it pierced. It hadn't hurt at all, he told him. Bill said he'd get one too, but only if George went with him. George agreed.

"Those boys have a fresh mouth," Ms. Higgins said.

"Eh, forget the pills," Charlie said. "What do I need 'em for, I'll be dead soon."

"Oh stop it," I said.

RETURN
TO
THE
DIRT

1

Smoking pot is how I've managed to waste most of my time. I'll lay with my back against the gritty roof shingles and look up at the stars, just wondering what my little place is in the universe. Nothing seems so important once you've wrapped your mind around your sheer cosmic insignificance. The entire planet barely holds any weight in the vastness of the universe; what great things could a mere earthling hope to accomplish as one of its ten zillion temporary guests?

This is the kind of insight that will save a guy a lot

of stress and pressure. It's also the kind of insight that kept me unemployed, single, and sleeping in my childhood bedroom for thirty-five years, in no danger whatsoever of achieving anything with my terrestrial life. And with my dad's life insurance money running out fast, my future looked as bleak and finite as the rest of the universe. And if you're wondering right now: Chris, doesn't it get old? Yes. It sure does.

On a whim of stoned epiphany—which typically fuels my most ponderous creative inspirations—I thought I'd turn over a brand new leaf. I typed a combination of words into my search engine I'd never typed before—job opportunities. I had this tangy sensation like I'd done something naughty.

With the recession and everything—the depression, if you asked most people—there were few results, and even fewer I could see myself doing for forty hours a week. The only jobs I managed to dig up were a few entry-level openings at none other than Flurf International, a bologna company whose reputation rivals the cigarette conglomerates.

My dad told me once, the best jobs centered

around doing work no one else could stomach. He made a decent living cleaning up Port Authority bathrooms, because very few other people wanted to do it. And with good reason. One morning, someone saw the bottoms of his boots poking out from under a toilet stall door and called the police. They found him on his knees and knuckles with his face in an un-flushed toilet. He'd been stabbed. They never caught the killer, who'd made off with no less than his lunch money.

Whatever stigma an entry-level job at Flurf International might carry, I probably wouldn't get stabbed and dunked in a toilet. So what the hell, I thought. Look out world, here comes Chris.

With my underwhelming work history, zero qualifications, and no references, I completed the form in milliseconds. Pertinent proficiencies: none. Political affiliations: none. Hobbies and/or interests: none. I couldn't have made myself seem like more of a simpleton. The truth is, I wasn't really trying, only trying to convince myself that I was trying. I knew I was un-hirable. At least I could tell mom I applied for a job. I'd make sure she was sitting down when I told her, she'd probably faint.

But I was the one who nearly fainted. The hiring department called me back the very next day and said they wanted me in for an interview. And when they decided they liked me and told me where and when to show up for "new employee orientation class," I was stunned. I walked out of the hiring office that day in a daze. Flurf International, a substantial corporation, wanted me as an employee? Wanted to offer me "opportunities for growth and advancement"? Me? The implications shattered my comfortable state of complacency. What in the world was happening to this little earthling?

So here I was, at the crossroads. I'd been given an incentive to change my ways. To clean up my act and start living like a real adult. To make a living. And eventually, a chance to move out of my mom's house and get my own place. To finally move out of my mom's house. Just thinking about it was so surreal I could barely believe it.

That day, in the hallway of the hiring office, I resolved to myself that I'd give it my best try. And in a move of faith that betrayed my DNA down to the last gene, I went home and flushed the rest of my stash down my mom's pink, porcelain toilet. Chris was starting anew next Monday morning. The nation's newest member of the workforce.

By the first new employee orientation class, I hadn't smoked pot in nearly a week, and I was feeling pretty chipper. I was there early, just sitting by myself in the chilly, institutional grey classroom, awaiting my destiny. The woodgrain plastic desks and painted cinderblock walls reminded me of high school, and I realized just how long it had been since I'd ventured outside my comfort zone. Naively, I fantasized about my professional potential. I came up with corporate-sounding titles for my future positions: District Logistics Manager, Director of Assets Management, etcetera. I was plotting my own success story.

Other new-hires began filing in, and the chairs all filled with faces unaccustomed to the morning. Most of them baggy, unshaven, and clinging to styrofoam coffee cups.

There were twelve of us in all, in four rows of three seats. I sat in the back row next to a portly fellow named Derek, and a shaggy bohemian named Brian. Once we started chatting, it seemed fitting we'd sat together. We were back-row types of guys; unexceptional, mid-thirties bachelors, each as surprised to be there as the next. Even Brian, who seemed convinced that any form of employment was "mind control," recognized his luck in being offered a paying job. Most notably in common, we were all potheads who'd recently quit to take a stab at the working world.

Our instructor came into the room carrying a big binder labeled *Itinerary*. He stood at a little podium and opened the binder and flipped a few pages and cleared his throat.

"Welcome, new employees," said our instructor. "I'm Clyde Everett, New-hire Orientation Director for Flurf International. Before we begin, a little about myself. I've been with Flurf for fifteen years. I started in preparation, moved to merchandising, and then to management. As you can see, there are plenty of opportunities for advancement in this growing company, and with hard work and dedication, you can build a great career with us as well."

A few of the newbies nodded appreciatively.

"To begin, I'll be playing a video presentation introducing you to something you're all quite familiar with, but likely haven't had the chance to fully understand. This video is entitled: Food: Why Flurf is Food."

He turned down the lights and started the video, which was projected onto a plastic sheet on the wall.

The video was nearly too cheap to take seriously. It was a kind of salesy, chiropractor's office-pitch designed to convince us that Flurf bologna was indeed real food. Being a former pot smoker, all I could think about was how utterly bizarre and trippy it was. Forty-five minutes later, here's what we'd learned:

Food is comprised of protein, carbohydrates, and fat. Water, vitamins, minerals, all those are in there too, but the calories that make up any meal are comprised of protein, carbohydrates, and fat; seven, seven, and nine calories, respectively. So if there were any preconceived notions about the quality of the product, remember that Flurf has a macronutrient ratio of ten grams carbohydrate, five grams protein, and eight grams fat. It even has fiber —one gram per serving. Flurf bologna is indeed, and meets all the necessary qualifications to be considered viable, edible food. You can totally eat it, and people totally eat it all the time.

"Dude," Brian whispered out of the corner of his mouth, "this whole smoke and mirrors game is full of subliminal mind control tactics." He'd whispered sentiments like this through the entire video, giving the whole presentation the feel of a high-school detention.

"They think I don't notice, dude, but I see all. My mind is a psychic planetary force."

"If my mind is what they want," I said, "it's a fair price to pay to move out of my mom's house."

"Don't look at the screen," Brian said. "Focus somewhere else. Focus on the wall or something, so it looks like you're watching, but don't look. Or you'll be inundated with subliminal suggestions. Not everyone can catch them like I can."

"I should've worn my tinfoil hat," I whispered.

"What?"

"Nothing."

The instructor turned up the lights and walked back to his podium and opened his itinerary book.

"Any questions about the video?" he asked. "No? Good. Now that we're all clear what food is, this next video highlights the merits of Flurf, and explains the mission statement of our company—to feed the world at all costs. Then, we have a special surprise for all of you."

He started the next video and turned down the lights and went back to sit off in the corner. The gist of the second video was this: With the world the way it is nowadays; overpopulation, food shortage, widespread disease, malnutrition and starvation, the old benchmarks of quality-food need desperately to be reevaluated. Food is calories. Maybe it's difficult these days to come across a grass-fed filet mignon with a side of organic asparagus spears, but you know what? If you aren't such a picky-pete, you can generally get yourself a nice Flurf sandwich. And for ten dollars a day—the price of a cup of coffee—you can provide a slab of Flurf bologna for a starving third-world family. Maybe it isn't the nutritionists, the environmentalists, and the vegans that have the answers to the world's real problems anymore. The real answer, argue as they all may, is Flurf International.

While the narrator fed us these facts, the screen played a pleasingly hypnotic display of dancing molecules, presumably proteins.

"I'm starving," Derek said. "Those Flurf molecules are making me hungry. Isn't that weird?"

"Mind con-tro-lio," sang Brian, elbowing me.

"Let's just pay attention, guys," I said. "They might quiz us or something."

"I told you, don't look at the screen," Brian said. "I knew it. You've been mentalized, dude."

"Gimme a break."

"You guys hungry?" Derek said. "I'm for seriously starving."

"Subliminal suggestion, dude. Believe me, you're the least starving person here."

Derek folded his hands over his belly. "How rude."

"I'm just saying..." said Brian.

When the video was over, Everett turned up the lights and walked back to the podium.

"Any questions about the video? No? Good. We

have a special surprise waiting for all of you, but first, a little history." He flipped a few pages of his itinerary book.

"It all began in a small garage, the modest beginnings of a company destined to change the way the world eats forever. The lone employee, son of an environmental engineer, had a food processor and a vision. That vision was, every man, woman, and child on the planet, enjoying a bologna sandwich. And that vision was the seed of the company that would one day become Flurf International. And that man was CEO Trevor Tannery. And now, on behalf of CEO Tannery, I'd like to present you all, fledgling employees with big dreams for the future, with a nice Flurfwich, compliments of Flurf International."

Right on cue, the double-doors to the hall swung inward and an unenthusiastic black dude pushed in a rolling cart with a large deli tray. The room filled immediately with the preservative tang of Flurf.

"Everybody enjoy a Flurfwich," Everett said. "Eat, and be filled."

Derek stood right up, patting his belly. He looked quizzically around the room. No one else seemed to be so hungry.

"That's the spirit, Derek," Everett said. "Enjoy a nice Flurfwich."

"Well, I suppose I'm obliged," said Derek.

Brian leaned and whispered: "Derek is dangerously vulnerable to hypnotic suggestion."

"Maybe he's just hungry. I'm hungry too, I'm just not into Flurf. Too salty. And rubbery. And strange."

"Not to mention the burps. My sister always has Flurf burps. They'll raise the dead and kill them again."

"Come on, everyone," said Everett. "Show some support for the product, you're part of the team, aren't you?" He was looking at Brian and me when he said it. Chairs creaked as the others got reluctantly from their seats. Brian and I looked at each other. There was no avoiding it. We got up and joined the others around the deli spread.

"This feels more like an initiation than a special surprise," I said.

"Chew carefully, dude" Brian said. "If you feel anything crunchy in your mouth, don't swallow it. It could be a microchip nano mind-controlling device."

"Delicious," said Derek, wolfing down huge bites. "I love Flurf. You know who else does? Twinkie."

"Twinkie?" I asked.

"My cat. He loves Flurf more than I do."

"Slow down," Brian said. "You heard what I said about chips."

"Chips? Who brought chips?"

2

I WOKE UP BEFORE THE ALARM on day two of orientation. Amazing how easily I hop out of bed in the morning since I quit smoking pot, just refreshed and ready to go. But the nights were when I paid for it; I'd just sit there completely sober, not knowing what to do with myself.

I weathered the boredom by watching nature shows on TV. The Wildlife Network was my favorite, lots of amazing animal footage. By the way, did it ever occur to you how much leniency the networks give to animals? We show them committing murder, having sex, all sorts of unsavory stuff you'd never want to see people do on network TV. Worse stuff, even. I watched a troop of chimpanzees track down a family of colobus monkeys and eat them alive, so add cannibalism to that list. You know who didn't seem to find it so offensive? Flurf. They sponsor the whole series, among many others.

We took a tour of Flurf's preparation and production facilities. They made us sign non-disclosure agreements, and our phones went in a cubby, to be returned upon our exit. No cameras were permitted anywhere, not even security cameras. This, they explained, was for concern that any of Flurf's technology would get into the hands of competing companies, which could compromise their share of the marketplace. Flurf's preparation and production processes were sophisticated, they told us, and needed to be carefully guarded to protect the value of the product.

"Dude," Brian said, reluctantly signing his form, "I smell royal, major league mindfuckery."

"I smell a paycheck. I'll sign whatever they give

me."

"The devil-may-care type, huh? Reckless, dude."

"Whatever," I said.

The instructor punched a code into the security keypad—which I happened to notice was 3,5,8,7,3, numerical for "Flurf"—and the doors to the preparation area opened onto a large chamber. We walked out on a grated skyway between the mouths of giant, metallic vats bubbling with thick, pink sludge, pouring steam into the humid air. The sludge, explained the lady leading us down the platform, was Flurf bologna in the making. I could see why nobody wanted cameras in there—it looked about half as appetizing as the finished product. Not surprisingly, Derek thought differently.

"Oh man," he said. "I could jump into one of those vats and just eat and eat." He patted his belly.

Brian cringed. "Ugh, you're an animal."

Steepling her fingers, the guide began her presentation. "Well I'm sure you've all wondered at some point how Flurf got to be called Flurf, and I'm here to show you there's more to it than a cute name. These are Flurf's top-secret atomization vats; where the ingredients are mixed into the uniform paste that eventually becomes everyone's favorite sandwich stuffer. Now, listen closely."

She grabbed a lever protruding from the control console of the vat and pulled it. Then...

FLUUUURFF!

Oily bubbles rose to the surface, popped, and wheezed. A hot breeze passed over us, like a massive Flurf burp, rustling my clothes and curling my nostril hairs. The ripples in the Flurf folded in on themselves and the goop's surface returned to normal.

"Did you hear that funny sound? I know you did. That's the sound that gives Flurf its name. The Flurfers send a superheated blast through the paste, giving it that uniform, perfectly mixed consistency it's known for. It also sterilizes the mixture, ensuring a healthy and hygienic product with a long shelf-life. The sound of our Flurfers is the heartbeat of Flurf International. We're so proud of it, we named the product after it."

"Dude, these vats are radioactive holocaust machines."

"Have you indeed ever seen a radioactive holocaust machine?"

"Just did, dude. Hope you wore your lead jockstrap."

"You're wearing a lead jockstrap?"

Truthfully, if he had been, it wouldn't have surprised me much. I was starting to believe Brian was fairly bananas.

After completing new-hire orientation, Brian, Derek and I were placed together in production. It was a big, white, Flurf-redolent lab with twelve air-compressed tubes from the preparation area snaking down from the ceiling like vines. On each tube was a valve. You fit the bologna skin on the end of the valve, pull the lever to fill it with hot Flurf, twist the end, cut it off, and roll it down the chute to the packaging area. You could always tell when a new vat got tapped; the Flurf came out like a firehose, and you had to go easy on the lever.

Of course the work didn't match up with my new fantasies of big-shot corporate success, but I knew that wouldn't come overnight. Meanwhile, the only part of the job I found really unpleasant was the smell of the bologna, which seemed to work its way into my pores. This only made me more motivated. I wanted to climb my way up the ladder and get out of the factory and into an office, like Mr. Everett had. I often renewed my resolve to stay on the straight and narrow until things panned out. I stayed focused. I had a clear vision for the future.

In the meantime, we made bologna from eight to six with a one-hour lunch break in between, which we usually took together in the cafeteria. Derek ordered a double Flurfburger every day, and that's only because a triple wasn't on the menu. Brian usually ate chips, and I had chocolate milk. If you didn't like Flurf, your options were drastically limited.

"Monotonous work is a tactic to foster mental conditioning," Brian said. He'd said that quite a few times lately. There was probably some truth in it, but what difference did it make? We had to work anyway, didn't we?

"Who cares?" I said. "We have to do it, so why complain about it?"

"Life is about more than work," Brian said. "Maybe these corporate goons don't get that, but I do."

"I agree," said Derek. "Life is about enjoying life, for seriously."

"All I've had up until now is life," I said. "I've front-loaded my life with life. I figure now I have a lot of work to do."

"So you're gonna work your ass off for the rest of your life?" Brian said. "Then what?"

I had no reply for that. I was stunned, actually. Brian had just disturbed a delicate balancing act in my brain I'd been performing successfully for more than a month. The question was one I'd asked myself countless stoned and introspective nights, and I'd never had an answer to it. No answer at all.

Here's the thing. My decision to turn things around had never been based on any deeply understood or conclusive revelation, only boredom and some ephemeral wave of interest I'd been trying to ride as long as I could. And now he had to ask me the big question. Why work? Why care? Why bother? With your infinitesimal presence in the universe, why?

"I'll tell you who's a real company man," Brian

went on. "Derek over here. Just look at him. He's practically made of Flurf."

"Guilty as charged," Derek said. "You are what you eat, right?"

Brian chuckled and got up from the table. "I'll be back in five," he said. "Maybe ten." He headed out towards the bathroom. I watched him disdainfully as he left. He'd really rubbed me the wrong way with that comment of his. It hadn't been on purpose, of course, but he'd sure fingered my self-destruct button. I'd try to forget it.

"The guy ought to have his prostate checked," I said. "He's in the bathroom constantly."

Derek took awhile to reply. He was chewing. "He isn't pissing," Derek said. "No one pisses that much. You know what he's doing."

"What's he doing?"

"You can't tell?"

"What is it?"

"He's toking up."

"What? You think?"

"Oh yeah, totally."

"How do you know?"

"I can tell. He looks lit up every time he gets back from his little bathroom trips. He's probably got a one-hitter."

"I hope not, he's going to get himself fired."

"Maybe he secretly wants to get fired."

"No way, why would he want that?"

"Some people just can't get out of their own way. He's one of those guys. He'll never cut the shit, believe me."

I can't explain what happened to me just then. I was electric with frustration, like something had been triggered in my brain. I thought I was just irritated with Brian's weak will, but no, that wasn't exactly it. I was imagining how much sweeter that chocolate milk would taste if I were high too. My mouth went dry and I felt my heart rate quicken.

"Dammit, Derek, the three of us just couldn't hold it together, could we?"

He looked confusedly at me while he chewed. "Huh?"

"Seriously, is it really that hard for the three of us to just not get high? If Brian can't even make it, what the hell are our chances?"

"It's just him though," he said. "We're still good. Aren't we?"

"I thought we kind of had a thing going, that's all. Solidarity, you know?"

"So what are you saying, just because he can't do it means we all screwed up?"

"I don't know anymore."

Brian noticed us examining him as he came back to the table. Now that I was paying attention, it was obvious that Derek was right. Brian was high.

"What?" said Brian.

"Where have you been doing it?" I said.

"Doing what?"

"We know, Brian."

"You know what?"

"You're off the wagon."

"Nah, dude, I'm good." He looked into his bag of chips.

"It's obvious," Derek said. "We're not dumb, you know."

"I can beat the tests, dude, I know what I'm doing. I have these pills, and if you take one a half-hour before—"

"But where? Where can you spark up and nobody can smell it?"

Brian paused. "I found a place," he said.

"Yeah, I gathered that much, but where?"

"Why? You're not thinking of..."

"Fuck it," I said. "Where is it?"

The look on Brian's face had changed from guilty to eager.

"Seriously?" said Derek.

"You coming?" I said.

He just stood there a moment, then slapped down his Flurfburger. "Well, fuck it," he said.

It was a well-ventilated maintenance room behind the first-floor stairwell in the rear of the building, not far from the nook with the bathrooms. We called it the crawlspace, but there was plenty of room for the three of us to pass a joint back and forth and blow the smoke through Brian's fabric softener sheet-filter concoction. All you had to do was get there without being seen and you could hide out as long as your absence raised no eyebrows. Three hits in, the shadows from the slats in the air vent were like tribal tattoos on the wall. Five hits, and it occurred to me that the insulated I-beam overhead was preventing the building from crashing down on me, and I was overwhelmed with reverence. I missed the hyperbaric thoughts and sensations, and after so much time sober, I was primed for them. Brian let us use his eyedrops, and we all headed back to the production area ready to finish the day stoned to the gills. I was trying to decide then, while I packed my next bologna, why the hell a place would prohibit its employees from smoking marijuana. It made everything so much more enjoyable. Maybe Brian was right. Maybe the forces of mind-control were at odds with us after all.

"So those pills," I said. "They really work?"

Right away it became a daily thing. For weeks, we spent half of our lunch breaks in the crawlspace and the other half cramming junk food into our faces. If drug testing came up in conversation, we simply changed the subject and pretended there was no way it would happen to us. The typical addict's way of dealing with problems is to ignore them, and that's just what we did, for almost a full month of stoned regression. The initial blast of it, the full-bore high,

steadily gave way to common stonedness. Pretty
soon, those old sentiments were crawling back into
my thoughts, the ones that tried to tell me I was
wasting my time trying to live like everyone else, just
working my way into oblivion. What was the point?
Just toke up, relax, and ride this life out in comfort.
Why strive? Why deprive yourself? It's only a matter
of time before we're all worm food.

Through it all, and I'm not sure how, I managed to
keep that little pilot light of faith burning dimly.
There were moments I nearly gave up and quit my
job, yet this little sober angel on my shoulder always
told me to stay. But as far as ambition went now, I
was resigned to remain a simple bologna packer.

One night I lit a joint and lay under the stars the
way I always had, but the sky just didn't look the
same to me. I looked up at the seven stars of the big
dipper. The closest star in the group is fifty-eight
light years away, and the furthest is one hundred
twenty-four; I'd always thought it was ridiculous to
associate them with one another at all, but now it
truly had no depth. All it was now was a dipper. The
sky might as well have been a TV screen, and the

stars, an episode of the latest pop-American sitcom. Whatever magic chemicals the pot squeezes out of your brain weren't there anymore, only the sluggish side-effect that accompanies them. Just the way it had been when I'd quit the first time. In a mere month, I'd managed to become a stoner again.

I'd always thought pot was the solution to life's doldrums and anxieties, at least until I'd gotten hired at Flurf. But there's a sneaky, cumulative side-effect to drugs. Once the spacey nonsense is wrung out of your brains from years and years of use, all that's left is an underachiever on his mom's roof, looking up at the stars like an asshole.

The foggy realization came to me that I was sabotaging myself, yet again. I needed to get off my ass, and while I was at it, off the roof and back on my feet.

I made a private oath that night, a promise to the universe I haven't broken to this day. I had a good thing going. And I would never again do anything to stand in the way of my career. My job came first, before any personal desires, personal feelings, or personal anything. I'd take every opportunity I could get, and I'd never quit. I was back on the wagon. Look out, world, Chris is back.

3

BACK AT FLURF, Derek and Brian were still up to their old lunchtime tricks, but I'd told Derek I was back off pot, and this time, for real. Brian accused me of having been mind-controlled and subscribing to elitism and all that, and I told him if I ever needed a career counselor, I'd ask him for his opinion. As stoned as he was, my sarcasm wasn't lost on him, and things were never the same between us. Soon after, I started spending my lunch breaks alone. It was the right thing to do to avoid temptation.

Everything went smoothly for a week, until the day I got the bad news. I was sitting on one of the hard plastic benches in the break room reviewing my protocol handbook when the door swung open and in bounded Brian, looking uncharacteristically shaken up. His normally half-masted eyelids were rolled up like spring-loaded blinds. I'd never seen him like this before.

"Dude..."

"What?"

We just stared at each other for a moment. He didn't seem to know what to say next. A few of the packaging guys peered disinterestedly from behind their Flurfwiches, then went back to eating.

"Dude, come outside a minute."

"What is it?"

"Just come on."

I got up and followed him out into the hall. His eyes were darting around crazily and he couldn't stand still.

"Relax, man. What is it? You on uppers or what?"

He drew a deep breath. "Me and Derek smoked some crazy shit in the crawlspace. Someone was outside the stairwell, so we freaked out and decided to go upstairs and sneak back through the preparation department. So we're out on the skyway and Derek says he's starving and he leans over and tries scooping up some Flurf, and his leg goes over the thing and he falls in the vat!"

"What? Where is he now?"

"In the vat!"

"Is he okay?"

Brian appeared even more uneasy. "I was so high I didn't know what to do. I went back to help him and I figured I'll turn off the thing, I don't know. I started messing with the controls. And then the Flurf thing went off."

"What? When did this happen?"

"Like just now, dude. What do we do?"

For a second, my body wouldn't even respond. Then I got ahold of myself and started running. Brian ran behind me. I remembered the code to the preparation area and punched it into the security console. We'd be in trouble if we got caught in here, but foremost in my mind was Derek. *God, I hope he's alright.*

It was just the two of us on the elevated pathway between the vats. Brian stopped me at Vat Six.

"It was here, dude. He just went right over. Oh my god, his mouth was open, you could see the stuff rush in his mouth."

"Maybe he got out. Maybe he's alright?"

"I saw him go down when the Flurfer went off. He sank like a rock."

"We have to tell someone," I said. "What does it say in the procedurals for this?" I opened my handbook and started flipping through.

"We can't, dude!"

"We can't just leave him in there!"

"We can't get him out either. He's Flurfed, dude. He's Flurf! Derek is Flurf."

I stared into the churning meat. You could feel the heat coming off from the last Flurf. Little bubbles still bursting on the surface. Brian was right, there was no getting Derek out of the vat. He was gone.

We were silent walking back to the break room. We sat back down at the table. Brian was wringing his hands together.

"So what the hell are we supposed to do?" I said.

"We can't just not report it. He fell in. It was a terrible accident, but it wasn't your fault."

"It was his fault he fell in there, dude. But I'm the one that hit the Flurfer. They'll think I murdered him, dude. I'll end up in prison! I'll get the electric chair!"

"Alright, quiet down. That was an accident too, you had no reason to hurt him."

"They'll drug test me, dude, they'll never believe me. Even if they believe me, I'll still get fired. I'll never get a job again!"

"Well let's think about this. You have those pills, you said."

"They don't work, dude, get real. Maybe if you smoked like once or twice, but I smoke all day, every day."

"Someone died, it's not like nobody's going to notice!"

Just saying it felt so bizarre. I couldn't believe Derek was dead. Brian paused. His expression swiftly changed from freaked out to assertive.

"Then when both of us get fired for failing our drug tests, we can sit at home with no money again and feel happy we did the right thing. And neither of us ever have to worry about working again, because nobody will hire us."

"First of all, what do you mean both of us? I had absolutely nothing to do with this."

"If you tell, you do. I'm not going down alone, dude."

"I quit. I haven't smoked for over a week."

"It's in your system for two weeks, and you know that, friendo."

We stared coldly at each other. It was clear what he was getting at.

"I know you want to do the right thing, dude. But the right thing is the wrong thing right now. Derek lost. We don't all have to lose."

I sighed and crossed my arms.

"Derek lived alone in a room," he went on. "He had no family, only his stupid cat. We're the only people that know he's gone, and we're the only ones that are going to know. Because if I go down, dude, I'm taking you with me."

4

IT USED TO FREAK ME OUT to imagine that we're all made of the same stuff. I mean everything; planets, stars, people, animals, vegetables, bacteria, viruses, all the same stuff. You could extract the molecules out of any star in the sky, take it apart, and put it back together to make an exact, working duplicate of any of us. Even the intangible stuff: thoughts, emotions, consciousness. They're all somehow made of stuff. And if you wanted to, you could take any of that stuff back apart and squeeze it together in some cosmic cheesecloth and you'd have yourself a star.

Now sober, my thoughts were grounded. I had time to think about what happened to Derek and all the implications. I don't know why it took so long to occur to me, but I realized that Derek would soon be squeezed into a thousand sandwiches. Choosing not to come forward about the accident meant more than just negligence. It meant people were going to eat him.

The thought of it made me want to light up a joint and just float away. But I'd made a promise. I'd come this far, and I wasn't about to give in. Plus, once I'd been clean for a full two weeks, that jerk wouldn't have anything left to hold over my head.

The next morning, Tom, the floor supervisor, walked over to Brian and me just as we were getting ready for our lunch hour.

"Guys, I could be wrong, but wasn't there another one of you new guys?"

"The fat guy?" Brian said. "Yeah, I just figured he quit."

Tom looked at me. I couldn't make eye contact with

him, so I just looked down at my work.

"Figured he quit," I said.

"Why would he do that?" Tom said. "Seems unlikely he'd quit a perfectly good job."

"Maybe he just didn't jive with the mind-control of corporate America," Brian said. "Who knows?"

"You haven't heard from him at all?"

"We didn't even really know him," Brian said.

"Nope," I said. At least that much was true.

Tom just stood there a minute, nodded, then walked away. I felt a bead of sweat roll into the small of my back.

"How long are we supposed to keep this up?" I said.

"What do you mean, how long? He quit, that's all."

I didn't reply.

"Dude. I know you want to do the right thing. I get it. Guys like you want to do the right thing all the time. But trust me. There's no reward in it."

Maybe he was right, I didn't know. But it felt totally wrong.

All the new employees were to gather in the

auditorium for a speech from the seldom-seen CEO, Trevor Tannery. I sat in the back row, and when Brian got there, he went ahead and sat next to me, leaving one seat in between. I don't know what he was thinking—it's not like I wanted to hang with him anymore. The guy accidentally murdered our friend and now he's basically holding me hostage. He's probably just keeping a close eye on me, I thought. Keep your friends close and your enemies closer. Well, I had my eye on him too. At 10:00 am sharp, the CEO came out on stage.

Trevor Tannery wasn't how I'd pictured him. He was tall and muscular, with extravagant, wavy, platinum hair and severe features. His suit looked custom, but he seemed to wear it like a uniform. He also didn't look like a man who ate much Flurf. He looked more like a man who ate his competitors. He spoke in a southern accent, and with such a deep, resonating tone that he probably could've gotten away without using a microphone at all.

"I'd like to personally welcome you all to Flurf International. As the world's finest and fastest-growing bologna company, we're excited to hire new employees to help us meet the needs of our customers."

"Mind con-tro-lio," said Brian.

"Flurf all began with a vision. And that was every man, woman, and child having a bologna sandwich. With your help, we're making that dream a reality every day."

The newbies applauded half-heartedly.

"You might hear people talking about Flurf International in your everyday lives. Chances are, you already have. And unfortunately, they're not always such nice things. Now, it's human nature to criticize what we don't understand, and sadly, to shy away from the things that make us uncomfortable. Hunger, overpopulation, these are a couple of things that also make us uncomfortable. Unlike our naysayers, Flurf isn't afraid to address these issues, and we've built one heck of a business around it. We understand that inexpensive, plentiful food sources are absolutely crucial as the population continues to increase."

"Ugh," Brian said. "I'd rather starve."

"Humans lack the foresight to address our greatest

threats—again, it's our nature. But it's important for you all to fully understand the big picture. Naysayers harp on about organic food and evil factory farming, and local crops, etcetera. That's fine. But what we're doing here overshadows petty concerns. While they worry about antibiotics and hormones and spliced genes and other trivialities, we feed those in need. As employees of Flurf International, you can be sure that you're a part of the solution. So whether you're packing, preparing, mopping, taking inventory, or whatever at all you do for Flurf, be proud. Our mission statement. To feed the world at all costs. Thank you."

"Did you catch any of that?" Brian said. "I was covering my ears."

"Something about a company-wide drug test."

"Very funny, smartass."

That night was clear, a night I'd typically do some stargazing, but I was trying not to waste my time with that anymore. I didn't even put on the nature channel, too much to contemplate. Sober, I stared at some sitcom the rest of America was watching. I wondered if everyone else was chuckling along with the poorly-written dialogue and canned laughter. Hard as I tried to enjoy this regular guy-stuff, I couldn't manage a laugh of my own. But I'd keep at it, I thought. A zillion Americans couldn't all be wrong.

At around 8:00 my phone rang.

"Hello?"

"Dude, this you?"

"Brian? Where'd you get my number?"

"Something happened, man."

"What happened?"

"I was sitting here getting high and I just started thinking about what happened to Derek. And then I started thinking about his cat."

"Alright, so?"

"I thought I'd sneak into his place and see if he's alright. Maybe feed him. I don't know. I felt guilty. It's this weed I just got dude, it's like...sentimental weed.

"So what happened?"

"I was walking around his building looking for a way to get in, and when I went around the front, the cops were there. And I freaked out, and they asked me what I was doing and I didn't know what to say, so I said I was there to visit Derek. And they said he's missing, that's why they were there. And so they started asking me a whole bunch of questions. I was freaking out, dude."

"What did they ask you?"

"When was the last time I saw him, if he had any enemies, if he owed anyone money. I said no, the last time I saw him was at work. I dunno, dude, they took my info and everything. I'm just freaking out right now."

"We should just come clean, Brian. This is getting out of control."

"We can't, then the cops will know I lied. I'll be a suspect. Damn, I'm so stupid for even thinking about Derek's stupid cat. So stupid. Goddamn weed made me all sensitive and shit, it's like I mind-controlled myself or something."

"Just forget about it for now, we'll talk about it later."

"Yeah. Alright. I'll see you at work."

"Fine, bye."

I put down the phone and collapsed back on my couch. Suddenly I was gripped by anxiety, and with it, an almost overwhelming craving for pot, which hadn't happened since that time in the lunchroom.

Dammit, I didn't need this. I didn't need any of it. I wasn't even with him when this happened, I had nothing at all to do with it. Now I had to suffer through the stress of it? While I'm trying to change my lifestyle and do the right thing, this jerk is allowed to smoke all the weed he wants and sabotage my sobriety to boot? What the hell am I protecting him for?

I sat there and mulled it over until the sitcom's credits scrolled down the screen. For all I knew, Brian might be right after all, that there was no reward in doing the right thing. There was also no absolute guarantee I could pass a drug test if they decided to spring one on me now. I sat thinking about it for awhile. For better or worse, I made my decision.

5

IN THE MORNING, Tom told us we'd have a busy day. One of the vats was ripe and ready, and today they were tapping it. The Flurf would be coming down like lava, so we had to be ready to roll.

"Which vat?" I asked.

"Why does it matter?" Tom said. I sensed Brian looking at me.

"Just curious."

"Vat Six I think," he said, "not that it matters."

Of course it mattered. I admit, a lot of animosity

had worn off since the night before, and I woke up with roughly half the determination I had when I made up my mind. But now the idea of what we were about to do soaked sourly into my stomach. Brian seemed to sense something was wrong. He was paying very close attention to me, I could feel it.

"You alright, dude? You look a little pale."

"I'm fine."

"You sure?"

"Yeah."

"Is it about the vat? Dude, we'll have that thing empty in two days, then this whole thing is over. We're home free."

I couldn't believe this guy. The jerk missed every point there was to be made—what about the fact that we were about to make bologna out of a human being and send it to a thousand supermarkets? Home free in two days, he says. What a jerk.

"I gotta go," I said.

"Where are you going? We're about to get started here."

"Nowhere, don't worry about it."

"Dude, are you cool or what?"

I took off my apron and started walking to the exit. I felt Brian's eyes at my back as I went. Closer to the door, I picked up my pace.

"Dude, no!"

I heard him behind me and I sped up to a lope. He knew what I was up to. Just like that, the cat was out of the bag.

"Dude, don't be stupid, you're gonna get us both canned! You'll be sorry!"

I ran up the stairs and down corridor three, towards preparation. Halfway down the hall he'd become too winded to continue his tirade and I heard him wheezing. There was no discussion to be had anyway, I had my sights on the doors at the end of the corridor. Whatever the outcome, I was putting a stop to this right now. At the end of the hall I punched in the code, 3,5,8,7,3, and the magnetic locks released their hold on the doors.

Just as I pushed through, I saw a group of vat techs gathered halfway down the skyway, all looking up at the ceiling.

"Wait!" said Brian with his last gasp of air. I stopped, but it wasn't because of his insistence.

Nobody heard our entrance over the rumble of the tubular machine descending from the ceiling. It looked like some kind of giant woodwind instrument, moving over the vats like the claw of an arcade crane grabber. I hadn't noticed the machine during orientation, and none of the instructors had mentioned it to us.

"Stop it right there," came a booming voice, and the machine clanked to a stop above one of the vats.

The voice sounded familiar. When I saw one of the technicians step aside and pull back his facemask, I realized why. It was Trevor Tannery, the CEO. What was he doing here in preparation?

Brian's footfalls come to a halt behind me and his hand landed hard on my shoulder. "Dude, seriously, you can't—"

"That's fifty percent four-leggers by weight," one tech told Tannery. "Top 'er off and we'll call it a Flurf."

"Very good," said the CEO. "In the meantime, go ahead and tap Vat Six for production. I'll page Tom and let him—"

"Wait!"

The three techs and CEO turned their heads at once as I approached Vat Six. The CEO watched me with a wrinkled brow.

"You're one of the new production men, aren't you?" he said. "How did you get in here?"

I looked over my shoulder at Brian. His eyes were as wide as saucers. There was no turning back now. I was coming clean.

"Mister Tannery, I'm sorry to barge in, but there's something very important I have to tell you. It's about Vat Six. You can't tap Vat Six."

He watched me suspiciously.

"Why is that?"

I took a deep breath. I knew what I wanted to say, I just couldn't find the tact to say it. So I just started talking.

"Someone fell in there a few weeks back. A new employee, Derek. He was running through here and he fell in the vat. It Flurfed him. He's dead. And he's in there."

I didn't know how else to put it, but I'd said what needed to be said. I could only imagine what Brian looked like standing there behind me. I knew I'd opened a big can of worms, but it had to be done.

Mr. Tannery stepped in closer. "Are you sure? You saw this happen?"

"I wasn't there. But he was." I pointed at Brian.

The CEO shifted to Brian, whose eyes bugged out like ping pong balls. "Is this true?"

The three other technicians watched without expression. There was something about the way the CEO spoke now that commanded everyone around stop and listen.

Brian was wringing his hands. "He's a crazy dope fiend this guy," he said. "He's always making up crazy stories. It never happened. You should drug test him, you'll see."

"He's a liar," I snapped. "He's afraid for his job." I turned to Brian. "No problem feeding Derek to Flurf customers, huh? I'd like to see you eat some yourself!"

"He's crazy, sir. Don't listen to him, he needs help."

"Asshole!"

"Dope fiend!"

"You're the dope fiend!"

"Hold your horses," Tannery said. "Does anyone

else know about this?"

"Just Brian and me. We'd have told you earlier, it's just—"

"You say the fellow fell in there. About how much would you say he weighed?"

The impulse to argue between Brian and me gave way to confusion. We looked at each other. Did we hear him right?

"I'd say about two-fifty," Brian said.

"Closer to three hundred," I said. "Why?"

"Well, which is it? Two-fifty or three?"

Brian and I looked at each other.

"Maybe two-seventy-five?"

Tannery was doing some calculation on his handheld device. "Alright, we'll go with two-seventy-five."

The machine clanked into action and re-positioned itself over Vat Six. Tannery hit a button and a squeaking mass fell down the chute into the goop. Then another, writhing bodies and tails. It was a second or two before I realized what they were. They were rats.

"Let those Flurf awhile," said Tannery. "I'll add the

long pork to vats Three and Five, and we'll tap Six tomorrow."

Did he just say what I thought he said? I looked back at Brian, even he was stunned.

Tannery turned to us and saw we were both pie-eyed. Maybe Brian had been right. I never thought for a second anyone but the prep guys would be in there. And here was the CEO, staring at two trespassers, having blatantly broken into a top-secret area without permission. We were in trouble.

"I was trying to do the right thing, that's all," I said.

It had been the right thing to say. Tannery's expression softened.

6

IF YOU'D ASKED ME TEN MINUTES EARLIER
what would be happening right now, I'd have told
you the place would be flooded with security.
Instead, we seemed to be getting a personal
orientation course from Tannery himself. The matter
of Derek had quickly fallen to the wayside.
Apparently, Flurf's way to deal with a catastrophe is
to dump rats on it.

Just the three of us on the skyway, the CEO pacing,
he said: "My father was an environmental engineer

with the Federal Wildlife Commission. He said to me once: when there are too many mice, Trevor, add cats. So let me ask you this. What do you do when you've got too many cats?"

"Add dogs?" Brian guessed.

Tannery shook his head. "I thought you'd say that. Problem is, now you've got too many dogs. And soon, you've got too many rats again. Every effect has a side effect; ask any pharmacist, he'll tell you. The trick to treating the world's sickness is to create effects whose side effects are also desirable effects. You follow?"

I nodded. He went on.

"The only variable to produce my effect, like a gene in a strand of DNA, lies at the top of the food chain. In the natural order of things, the predators at the top need to be kept in check. I'll start where my father left off: Too many mice? Add cats. But what happens when you've got too many cats and the supply of mice are insufficient? The answer is a simple subdivision at the top of the food chain. At the top are the cats. And one step below that are now the other cats. The cats, at least the ones that know what's good for them, eat the other cats. The side-effect? Exactly what we needed in the first place. Fewer cats. Understand?"

"I think so," I said. "Sure," said Brian.

"The instinct to survive and reproduce is strong in humans. It surpasses all reason. We've known for many generations that the population would one day reach critical mass. I was the first man willing to put reasoning before instinct. And the answer was simply this: a simple subdivision at the top of the food chain."

"I don't quite understand the food chain thing," I said.

Tannery grinned. "I know you don't. So I'm going to show you." He reached back into his pocket and took out the remote control.

"Surplus people are everywhere. This bunch here are undocumented imports. They may look different, but they taste the same as everyone else. Side effect? National security."

He pressed a button and a ruckus filled the tube from the overhead machine. One by one, scream on scream, little brown people dropped from the mouth of the tube into Vat Five.

"What?" I said stupidly.

I watched as they tumbled in. When the surface of the Flurf was writhing with flailing arms and legs, Tannery flipped the switch, and the mass sucked down into the pinkish depths. I felt a wave of stinking heat breeze past my face. Bubbles rose to the surface and the mass was still again.

"They steal, rape and murder, and end up in prison for life, with the good taxpayers footing the bill. That's no way to pay your debt to society. So how do they make restitution? Feed the needy. Side-effect? Save taxpayer dollars."

He hit the button and in dropped people. There must have been fifty of them. The vat seemed to boil with score after score, all dressed in orange prison-garb, all fighting to stay above the surface. Tannery fired the Flurfers and they were sucked into the mix.

Brian and I looked at each other. *Is this for real?*

"They come in shipping containers from places like China and India, barge after barge of them. Their governments promise them better, more useful lives in America. Well, we send them back containers and containers of Flurf to feed the people. Side-effect, less people to feed in the first place."

The flow of people down the tube seemed never-ending. Maybe a hundred of them. Maybe more. One managed to hold onto the edge of the tube for a moment before losing his grip and falling in. Tannery had to pulse the Flurfers several times to keep the vat from overflowing. By the end of it, Vat Five was brimming with pink goop.

"Oh my God," Brian said.

"I knew you'd say that," Tannery said. "Strange, how no one ever has such spiritual sentiments while enjoying a Flurf sandwich."

The CEO approached Brian. "So, now that you know what you know, tell me this. I started this company as a young man in a garage with a couple of Cuisinarts. Do you believe a man with a poor judge of character could operate in such a business as I do?"

A poor judge of character? He's a goddamned... He's a radioactive holocaust machine.

"I guess not?" suggested Brian.

"That's no bologna," Tannery said. "And I know

bologna when I see it."

He seized Brian by the lapels and hoisted him up and over the guardrail. With a yelp, he splashed into Vat Five. He came up flailing, wheezing for breath. I backed away until my spine hit the opposite rail, my fight or flight response seemingly short-circuited. Tannery was standing at the console, watching Brian struggle to keep his head above the surface.

"Help me!" he gurgled.

"You're fired," Tannery said, and flipped the switch on the control board. The Flurfers flurfed. Brian's scream lasted only a fraction of a second, and I knew he'd just disappeared into the pink vortex. He was gone. He was Flurf.

Tannery turned to face me. There I stood, frozen with fear, my back pressed to the guardrail. The techs stood like sentinels at either side of the skyway. I was cornered. Below me bubbled the hot Flurf of Vat Seven.

7

I REMEMBER A COLLEGE COURSE I took during
my two-semester attempt at a higher education. It
was one of those bullshit one-credit courses I can't
even remember the name of. The professor was hell-
bent on scaring the shit out of us. The world, like any
other closed environment, has a capacity, he
explained. There's only a certain amount of people
that can live on earth. When the capacity is reached
and eventually exceeded, what would happen? He
believed the whole world would collapse at once, like

a stage with one too many performers. Inevitably, a single man or woman would be the proverbial straw that broke the camel's back.

I raised my hand and disagreed. Could the world truly approach capacity? If we got even close, wouldn't people also die off at a proportionate rate?

Anyway, the news these days seems to be filled with exactly that—mass die-offs from disease and starvation, notably. The ongoing epidemics in Africa, perverted versions of the flu widespread in South America, mutated childhood diseases defying vaccinations in America. As insistent as we are on reproduction, the planet continues to shake us off like fleas. I still don't believe the earth's population could ever reach critical mass, but that's because the faster you pour us on, the faster we seem to spill over the edge, like an overflowing bathtub. But is this really any more comforting than Mr. Simm's theory?

Years go by pretty fast already. The idea of people expiring like mayflies only makes the human experience seem less important to me. Being a person is just the strangest thing to do before you return to the dirt.

So that's how I got my job in quality control at the world's biggest bologna company. I kept my promise to stick with it no matter what. And for what it's worth, I think my dead dad would've been proud of me. He always said, the best jobs are the ones that are the hardest to stomach. My mom, she can't believe her son has finally grown up.

But I don't feel that way; like I grew up late. I feel like my long journey of drugs and leisure has come to its natural conclusion. It was what CEO Tannery told me that day he offered me the position. Sitting there in his office, smoking his cigar, feet up on his desk, he filled in the blanks for me, and no joint, no bong hit, no strain of nuclear marijuana could ever have made it clearer. I'm no longer tempted by drugs, no longer tempted by the promise of some secret wisdom therein. I lay sober on the roof of my own place now, looking up at the clusters of quarks in the sky, and I've never felt so strange, not even when I was stoned out of my mind. I picture being on some other planet, light years away, maybe some inconsequential little rock orbiting around the end of the Big Dipper, and looking up at the little blue dot of Earth. Maybe our sun is part of some silly constellation to this particular place, maybe the power cord of the Big Toaster. And I'll be damned, does it really make a difference what nastiness, what ugliness, what darkness goes on down here? Or whether I should work hard, or just ride this life out in comfort? Or what my little place really is in the universe? There's a reason these riddles are so illusive. Because if you pursue them to the edge of the cosmos and back, stars become rocks. Planets become dirt. And people become meat.

"Blend you up, young man, and you're made of the exact same stuff as everything and everyone else. And every one of those little atoms you're made of is billions of years old. They came from distant galaxies. They've been rocks, they've been plants, they've been animals, they've been human beings. They've been eaten by saber tooth tigers, velociraptors, and pterodactyls. They've been eaten by Cro-Magnon man, eaten by Neanderthals, eaten by modern man, and shit a hundred-million times. Every atom of your living body has always been there, and it'll live again and again, forever and ever.

That kid in Vat Six will live again. Our friend in Vat Five will live again. Every Mexican, Indian, Chinaman, Eskimo, convict, cow, pig, fish, horse, chicken; all the creatures that go into Flurf brand bologna, they'll all live again and again until the universe is reduced to quarks, and the quarks are reduced to nothing. The world, the universe, everything, it's all bologna. So eat. Eat and be filled."

Made in the USA
Monee, IL
15 June 2021